The Dancer's Spell

Peter Hassebroek

Upbound Solutions

Also by Peter Hassebroek

Upbound

Melange and Other I.T. Stories

Greenplays

Thylacine

The Dancer's Spell

The Dancer's Spell

Published by
Upbound Solutions, Whitby, Ontario, Canada

ISBN: 978-0-9866640-3-8

~ ~ ~ ~ ~ ~ ~ ~

www.peterhassebroek.com

The Dancer's Spell

*For the everlasting
spirit that is
Geoffrey*

The Dancer's Spell

The Dancer

"Can't say I've ever been moved by unveilings," I recall saying, as Max and I were about to enter the Musée Guimet.

"Indeed," my brother-in-law's glib response.

While I can appreciate his amusement now, twelve and a half years later, the events of that night and the months that followed continue to haunt me. But never so much as today, on this chilly, dark October morning at Vincennes on the outskirts of Paris, where I await with mixed emotion, as well as morbid detachment, the execution of Mata Hari. A long wait appears inevitable, equally so the impulse to reflect on what began that March evening in 1905. If I recall correctly, it was chilly outside the oriental art museum too, although warm inside.

Max and I checked our coats and hats and climbed the wide stairs to the third floor, squeezing into the crowded library filled with the elite of Paris. The murmuring and buzzing from the colourful and diverse assemblage of diplomats, military officers, artists, bankers, and other dignitaries created an anticipatory tension that seemed to auger a significant event.

The floor-level stage and distinct lack of elaborate decoration suggested otherwise. Vines wrapped around white Doric columns and pure white flower petals strewn about added a paltry touch of nature to the room's prim academic ambience. Various idols and other unusual art pieces, borrowed from the museum's collection no doubt, had been placed about the room. A haloed four-armed statue kept drawing anxious glances. Was this the object of all the fuss?

"The Hindu God, Siva," Max whispered, pointing at the statue.

"How pagan," I said. "Hardly worth missing the Eiffel Tower for."

"Wim, after tonight, you'll come to think of your precious Eiffel Tower as a hunk of dirty metal, an inverted bridge abutment."

"I take it then you are one of those counting the days till its dismantlement."

"Once again, you miss my—quiet, it's about to begin."

Candles were being snuffed out, one by one, until the only light came from a bowl of burning oil. It cast dim flickering glimpses of yellow upon the statue in a smoky dance uncannily synchronized to the melodic eastern music. The darkness exaggerated the thick incense as candle smoke rose upward and disappeared into the domed ceiling.

Four dark figures appeared. All women. All young, slender, and pretty. All with long, dark hair. All dressed in bare-shouldered full-length black gowns. They were chanting.

Each in turn danced in front of the statue, their lithesome movements intended to provoke a reaction from the inanimate object. Each concluded with a sorrowful retreat to the floor, rejection from the heathen god. There came a pause in the music, a dramatic silence before a lone woman emerged, barefoot, wielding a sword.

Her face was hard to make out, the features eclipsed by a rather garish headdress appointed with a dazzling quantity of jewellery. Even more gems on anklets, armlets, bracelets and an ornate metallic support garment. Other than a translucent gown, she wore little else. Her aura exuded sensuality and vulnerability; it made me uneasy.

Her dancing, deliberate and intense at the same time, incorporated every muscle in her body in ways I'd never seen before. Motions stirringly suggestive. That she was dropping her shawls while doing this eluded my notice until, to my horror, she unclasped a belt to release the last shawl, leaving her unabashedly naked.

"Max, this is outrageous," I said.

"Shh," he said, without looking at me.

Now the dancer began swaying her body sinuously in an unsymmetrical yet mesmerizing pattern. Back and forth. Back and forth. Arms and legs in constant motion. Faster and faster the rhythm went until exhaustion overcame her and she crumpled to the floor. The four women who had danced earlier covered the prone, unclothed form with a sarong. The dancer rose then, collecting and draping the thin cloth around herself with aplomb.

"Captivating, no?" said Max, but I was too stunned to respond.

Re-lit candles re-illuminated the room and the dancer stepped toward her spellbound audience to accept her adulation. Now I could see the exotic loveliness of her face in better light. That diamond shaped mouth, the shining, lively eyes, the soft cheeks, the slender neck . . . then came an almost overpoweringly sickening feeling. I feared I was about to vomit. But instead I blurted out:

"Maggie."

Not loudly, but loud enough to draw glares from several people. Including Max, who was dabbing his forehead with his handkerchief. The dancer looked my way too but gave no sign of recognition as she took her final bows to a salvo of applause. When it stopped, Max's face expressed alarm.

"Wim, you're pale, what's the matter?"

"I think I know her, knew her."

"Who do you know?"

"Maggie, Margaretha," I said. "The dancer."

"You know Mata Hari," he said, snickering now, disbelieving yet enviously unsure. I nodded. Max lighted a cigarette and regarded me for a drawn out moment. "Impossible."

"Fine, don't believe me," I said, now wondering why his opinion mattered when, in fact, I dearly hoped I was wrong. I had to be wrong.

The bewitched audience unleashed another chorus of clapping and cheering, an appeal for more. Feeling claustrophobic, I hastened down the stairs, toward the exit, echoes of salacious applause ringing in my ears as I welcomed the bracing air and relative quiet of the mid-March night. I calmly put on my coat and hat.

A column of horse and carriage combos flanked the museum, angling off along two avenues. Drivers were leaning against them, sharing cigarettes and stories, conversations occasionally interrupted by a snort from their beasts. There were several well polished motor cars, their chauffeurs hunched over steering wheels, wearing superior expressions. A man walking an Alsatian approached one of the horseless vehicles with admiring curiosity. When the dog raised a back leg at one of the tires, the man jerked the chain. The dog, after a quick yelp, obeyed and moved on. At least Parisian dog owners have a sense of decency, I thought, but then wondered how long it would take before Max appeared.

Such a sociable dandy, my brother-in-law was probably finding old friends, or making new ones. People with whom he could exchange pretentious observations about the exhibition, conversations I wanted no part of. Not only was I ashamed at having attended such an event, it seemed I had discovered the ignominious fate of someone I once—then a disturbing possibility struck me: what if Max took it upon himself to talk to her? His disbelief notwithstanding, my admission would provide an excuse to approach her. And if he mentioned my name, what then? Worse, what if he called her Maggie . . .?

Oh, what was I thinking when I heeded my wife's suggestion to break up my trip home from Marseille to spend an evening with her younger brother? "A night in Paris would be good for you," she had said. I doubted she'd had this sort of entertainment in mind. If only I had gone straight to Gare du Nord for the next train to Amsterdam instead. Then I would be sitting in my favourite room by the canal, in my favourite chair, silently sipping a *borrel* by the fireplace. Cornelia would be reading a book or playing a game of Patience, our precious daughter, Antje, falling asleep on my lap.

Several puffs of smoke interrupted my brooding, accompanied by a familiar odour mix of tobacco and expensive cologne.

"Wim, I spoke with that dancer and she remembers you," Max said, but then chuckled before I could react. "No, just sporting with you, dear brother-in-law, I didn't talk to her. But tell me, when were you ever in the East Indies?"

"What are you talking about?"

"Come on Wim, don't pretend, not with me. This Maggie girl, the one who was dancing. Turns out she's from Java."

Aside from the dusky features, the woman had not appeared foreign to me. But that made the possibility she was not Maggie more viable. The room had been dark, after all. And the chance of encountering a girl I knew from sleepy, provincial Leeuwarden, dancing in Paris without her clothes on, was preposterous.

"So you believe me now?" I said. Max shrugged so I added, "Well, if she is from the East, then it's obviously not her."

"And who would 'her' be?"

"Max, this is the first time I've seen this woman, or anything of this nature."

"No, I mean the one you did know. Maggie, or whoever."

"Oh. Someone from Leeuwarden."

"Must have been quite a girl."

"She was—Max, why did you take me to this indecent show?"

"Indecent?" he said, taken aback. "You can't be serious. Daring perhaps, but far from indecent. This is Paris in 1905, a new century."

"Well, this is Wim Brink, a man born in the old century."

"It's a pleasant evening," he said, now looking up at the blue-black sky. "Let's save some cab fare and walk back to my apartment."

"Fine."

We crossed the Seine and headed in the direction of the Eiffel Tower. Partway along the bridge, we came upon a pair of panhandlers, unshaven and huddled under dishevelled coats, an upturned hat in front of each. One man was lying down, the other sitting with his back against a railing. The rank smell of stale alcohol mixed with that of the river. Nauseating. I thought they were both sleeping, as they did not beg for alms when we passed. Ignoring Max's sigh of disapproval, I stopped to place a franc into each hat. The one sitting up stirred, stared down at the hat, and then up at me, with baiting eyes. He caressed his unclean beard.

"C'ést tout?" he said.

"Yes, that's all," I said, glaring back.

He chuckled. Except for a missing tooth and dirt on one side of his lips, his grin matched the lascivious arrogance I had witnessed at the Guimet. My spine stiffened, my blood heated, my fists clenched, the same instinctive call to violence that would come so readily in my youth in New York, and later in Leeuwarden. About to lash out at the panhandler, I felt Max's hand on my shoulder, as he said, in a raspy voice:

"What do you think you're doing?"

I brushed Max's hand away and kicked at the man's hat, which turned over. Several coins bounced off the bridge into the Seine. Echoing plinks and tiny plops. The panhandler's eyes glazed with fright, with hatred. His look reflected the self-disgust in my soul. Here I was, a mature, responsible businessman from the upper class, with a young family and successful career, acting like such a schoolboy. I pulled out a crumpled fifty-franc note, and threw it at him as I walked away. I glanced over my shoulder; the man hadn't moved, although the money had disappeared. Max said nothing about the encounter but I knew it disturbed him.

Further along the bridge, an artist in a well-worn grey smock was sitting on a small wooden crate, facing an easel with a canvas to which he was applying a brush with rapid, confident strokes. He was painting a river scene. Murky water, majestic buildings along the banks. A *bateau mouche* occupied by a young couple racing a barge loaded with shimmering black coal. Claiming artistic licence, he had squeezed in Notre Dame in the background. The lighting, though assisted by the Eiffel Tower, seemed insufficient for such painstaking work. He applied the finishing strokes—brush to palette, brush to canvas—with flair; his rapid, unbroken gesticulations a performance unto itself.

The painter dashed off a last symbolic stroke, grunted at the results, removed the painting from the easel, and then called out something, a name perhaps. A man in a dark jacket, smoking a cigar, took the finished piece and leaned it against a stack of about ten other paintings of the same scene.

"Now that's worth kicking into the river," Max said, and we both chuckled.

We continued on toward the Eiffel Tower. I slowed to admire the intricate metalwork up close; it was particularly stark from underneath. Yet my mood was off and that diluted my enjoyment; I'd appreciate it better in daylight. On we strolled into the Champ-de-Mars. The grass, benches, and flowerbeds with their budding bulbs were harder to see, easier to stumble into. We encountered fewer people too. Farther off to our left rose a large, magnificent golden dome I guessed to be the *Hotel des Invalides*. One of many points of interest dog-eared in my Baedeker, uselessly buried in my suitcase back at my brother-in-law's apartment.

My guidebook certainly could have helped identify the dark, subtly magnificent beige-brown concrete building at the end of the park. It looked so familiar, those Corinthian columns supporting a center section and second-floor balcony. Typically Parisian in its symmetry, probably eighteenth century. Only two storeys tall, and topped with a dark-grey roof, its width spanned beyond the confines of the park.

"Ah, the famous *École Militaire*," Max said.

"Yes, I know that," I said, my teeth chattering slightly.

And I did know that, recognizing it from my grandfather's postcard and favourite bookmark. "If you want to fight at school, I'll send you someplace you can learn to do so like a man, and get a good dose of discipline too," Opa Geert would say, putting whatever book he was reading down and producing the picture. He did it often, whenever I came home with a black eye and bruised knuckles. Threats like that, along with his other strict measures, did not take long to turn the troublesome child he'd taken in into an obedient one. How I despised him at first; but how I grew to adore him, idolize him even. Standing there, next to Max, I once again appreciated the good intentions of that wonderful man who raised me after my father died.

"Napoleon Bonaparte attended this very school when he was fifteen," Max said. "Did you know it only took him one year to complete a two year program?"

"Why didn't you attend?"

"As a matter of fact," Max said, brushing off my sardonic tone, "my father hoped I would. But I'm a pacifist, you see. True, I was obligated for military service for Holland, but I managed to keep to a desk instead of shipping out to some place like the East Indies. Hmm, if I had then I wonder . . ."

"Wonder what?"

"Well, Mata Hari is from the East Indies, and so maybe I should have—oh, never mind."

Then two smartly dressed but clearly inebriated men stumbled back on a bench near us. One of them removed a flask from a coat pocket and took a drink; only the cleanliness of their clothes distinguished them from the panhandlers we'd run into earlier, in my eyes.

"After that performance, we need this," said the one with the flask.

The other nodded eagerly. "Have you ever seen anything like that?" He removed two cigarettes from a silver case, which he lighted. I took an instant dislike to them upon recognizing their faces from the audience at the museum. Their presence incited an emotion akin to jealousy.

"No," the first one said. "Never like that."

"I've been to many shows here in Paris, but this is of a different class altogether," the man with the cigarettes said, between drags.

"This promises to be a wonderful century."

"You see?" Max said, to me.

"See what?"

"No one thinks the show was indecent. Because it wasn't. It was art."

"Max, the woman was naked."

"Naked? Is that it? *Mon dieu*, half the paintings in the Louvre are of naked women. They weren't painted from the imagination, if you get my notion. And the collection at the Guimet, are you saying those sculptures, just because they're erotic, are not art?"

"Precisely."

His eyes narrowed and I could see he was struggling with how to continue his argument, or whether it was worth the trouble. I remained silent, happy in my obstinacy.

"At the risk of raining on your dogmatic parade, Wim, the woman was not actually naked. I thought she was at first, but I learned afterward she was wearing a body suit."

"What does that matter?" I said, sensing Max had said this more with regret than to appease me.

"It doesn't?"

"No, because everyone thought she was naked, and that was the impression she tried to give. It is the intent behind the act, more than the act itself that matters."

"I'm afraid you're confusing me."

"Think of an executioner on a firing line, when they give one of the men a blank but don't reveal which has it. Then each can deceive themselves into thinking they didn't kill their target because they did not fire a real bullet."

"My, my, Wim, you are in a bad way, aren't you? You know Cornelia would have—"

"Max, don't you dare sully my wife's name in this context."

Then Max's face took on a melancholic solemnity I'd never seen before.

"Wim, my sister was not raised in a convent. Her upbringing was as liberal as mine. She knows of the world and she's studied enough art to appreciate what we saw." I flinched but said nothing so he went on. "Or could it be this Mata Hari, or Margaretha, or whoever, is someone you once had a fancy for? Maybe you're just upset at seeing an old lover indelicately exposed to a roomful of strangers."

It took several deep breaths to summon the restraint used earlier with the panhandlers not to strike my brother-in-law. "I'm too tired for this, Max," I said, exaggerating my weariness.

"I'll hail you a cab."

I wasn't sure I had heard him right until he handed me a key.

"You're staying out?" I said.

"It's barely past midnight," he said. "You can join me if you wish, but there may be women where I'm going, and it does sound as if you'd favour sleep."

I did favour sleep, but sleep did not favour me. After a restless night, interrupted by unfamiliar noises and now forgotten dreams, I could no longer lie down. I rose just after six o'clock. It was a challenge to avoid stumbling in the darkness but I needn't have worried. Max's rhythmic snoring from behind his closed bedroom door did not miss a beat; sleeping the sleep of the innocent.

I spread apart a curtain to open one of the large double-paned windows. The electric streetlights cast a soft, strange luminescence on Max's Monet painting. And on his tasteful collection of knick-knacks from trips to Africa, which lined several shelves where one would ordinarily find books. Olive-coloured wallpaper made it all seem rather eerie. I looked out over the wrought iron railing onto a curving, dark and narrow cobblestone street and kept a vigil until the first glimmer of sunrise.

Boredom crept in before then and I decided to pack. That didn't take long, as I'd barely unpacked. I paced about then, intermittently picking up an African piece to study it, inspecting Max's collection of cigar boxes—all empty—or leafing through his thick stack of art magazines. The temptation to drop something to wake my brother-in-law crossed my mind occasionally. But instead I would return to the window to breathe in a lungful of damp air.

One by one, the lights were going out; the sun was taking over. The street—so busy late yesterday afternoon—was empty, save for a pair of unattended bicycles, a stray but well-fed tabby sniffing at closed doorways, and several deliverymen guiding carts drawn by mules: a bucolic village scene in the midst of this dissolute urban capital.

A wonderful aroma of fresh bread stirred my hunger. The source was a café down the street called *Chez Luc*. Its proprietor was leaning against the wall, leisurely smoking a cigarette. But then he dropped it to the ground, crushed it with his boot, and went inside, as if summoned. He re-emerged moments later to set out tables and chairs. I wondered who would want to sit outside on such a cool morning. Maybe it was just habit; maybe the furniture had to go out to make room inside. I dressed and scribbled a note for Max.

In the café, I took a small table at a window from where I could see my brother-in-law's building. No sign of activity whatsoever. My omelette and coffee came shortly, along with the puffiest croissant I'd ever seen, smelled, or tasted. I was afraid to touch it or even breathe on it, let alone spread butter or jam. The flaky pastry turned out more resilient than I expected and so delicious I gluttonously ate another.

A man and a woman vacated the table next to me, leaving behind a newspaper. I pushed my crumb-filled plate aside and grabbed the sheets, which were in a state of disarray I would never tolerate at home. As I reassembled them, an article about Mata Hari caught my attention. A review of last night's performance.

I had to look. I hoped—no, expected—to read a rousing critique, a condemnation that would satisfy even the good Reverend Schultens of my church in Amsterdam. After all, I could not have been the only offended spectator out of those hundreds. Even one opinion in accord with mine, I rationalized, increased the chance the performer was not my sweet Maggie.

I was wrong. About the condemnation, not the chance. The reviewer called Mata Hari exotic, called her dancing bold and evocative. The so-called critic—he sounded more like a publicity agent than an objective member of the press—heaped on plenty of other appreciative adjectives that were technically accurate, such as graceful, lovely, and original, but left out relevant ones such as lewd, obscene, and so on.

Reading this only increased the shame I felt for just being there. What would it do to my reputation as a moral, upstanding businessman if someone discovered as much? Never mind that I knew the performer. Possibly knew the performer. These thoughts were pressing on me when Max entered. He exchanged a greeting with the owner and several of the patrons, before taking the seat across from mine. He brought over a coffee for both of us, set them down, and then noticed the review.

"Aha," he said, with subdued triumph. He then pushed the paper aside and looked at me, wearing a contrite expression.

"Wim, I apologize for yesterday, for taking you to that performance. Entirely my fault. An honest mistake."

"Honest?"

"I expected something exotic, true, but nothing more than a unique Asian dance, not something so, well—"

"Lurid?"

"All right, if you wish," said Max, flashing a disarming smile. "And yes, when I discovered what it really was, perhaps my enchantment overpowered my good sense. Had I known beforehand, I'd have made other plans for us."

We touched cups together; I truly wanted to believe him. For Max was, at heart, a decent fellow. Pleasant to be around despite his questionable morals. He finished his coffee and let out a satisfied sigh.

"So now that that's out of the way," Max said, "tell me more about this Maggie girl."

"What does that have to—let's forget that."

"I disagree. I have some information that might interest you. After you went to the apartment, I met up with a friend."

"Don't tell me, Eric LaPlante." Max shifted uncomfortably before nodding. Then I saw the review I had read had been written by that very same person.

This Eric, a friend my brother-in-law had met in university, was an art journalist-critic, a petulant dilettante whose amorality and lack of height reminded me of Toulouse-Lautrec. I also suspected LaPlante of improper intentions toward my wife. Long before my marriage, he'd painted a stunning portrait of Cornelia. A painting I had admired at first but grew to loathe. Their friendship always bothered me. I disliked Eric and the feeling was mutual. I knew he would waste no time telling my wife where I'd been the night before to cause trouble.

"Don't tell me he knows I went with you," I said.

"Why no," Max said, with a slight tremble. "I never mentioned your name. It's not as if you're his favourite topic of discussion. You'd be the last person he'd have expected to come with me there." I nodded, satisfied. "Mata Hari, on the other hand, is a favourite topic of his. And he knows some things."

"Why on earth would I care what Eric would have to say about anything?" I said.

"Stop being this way. You're the one who claimed to know her. So listen, apparently the wonderful Mata Hari is married to an army officer, a Scottish fellow named MacLeod."

His eyes sparkled and he smiled as if expecting me to recognize the name. Instead, I was appalled. A married woman, dancing in such a way, in public. I shuddered at the idea but then realized the fact she was married wasn't the point.

"So?" I said.

"Excuse me, are you still reading that newspaper?" a voice behind us said.

"Yes," I said, before glancing up at the man standing over us. He had a dab of pastry icing in his silver beard. "I am."

"Very well," the man said. "But if you don't mind, may I have it when you're finished?"

"What? No, I mean, here, take it."

I shoved the paper at the man, accidentally tearing the review and creasing several pages. I heard his grumbling all the way to the other side of the café. The woman with him said something to him and then both glanced at me. I glared back.

"Forget them," Max said. "Don't you want to hear more about your girl?"

"She's not my girl," I said.

"Oh yes she is, or was. You were right and I must also apologize for not believing you."

"Max, the woman on the stage was not my friend. She couldn't be. If anything, I should be the one to apologize for deceiving you."

"You're sure Mata Hari's not your childhood sweetheart?"

"Keep it down," I said, "and yes, I'm sure."

He shrugged and then pulled out a napkin from a pocket with a sketch of a salon and dancing girl imprinted on it. He had to look closely to make out the handwritten notes on the back.

"All right. But consider this. Mata Hari's real name is Lady Gresha MacLeod and she was married in Amsterdam, and she's almost thirty—same as you. It must be her. Gresha is a variation on Margaretha, right?"

"Sure, it could be, yes."

"Of course it is. And Margaretha, well that's Maggie, no, to an American?"

"I was born in America. I lived there a few years. But I consider myself Dutch, thank you."

"And according to Eric, her biography is rather vague. Opaque, I think he called it but you know how pretentious . . . anyway he suspects she's manipulating the press."

I felt my face turn red. That sickening sensation from the night before returned, enhanced by a sudden funny aftertaste from the croissant. The Maggie I used to know would concoct fantastic autobiographies. Max smiled knowingly, as if reading my thoughts.

"Now you're trying to tell me this isn't the same girl you knew?"

Ah, if only I had just admitted it then. Who knows what might have happened other than it would have prevented so much lying. But denial seemed my only option with Max. Besides, I still held on to the hope it was a coincidence, despite that hope diminishing with each word of my feigned ignorance.

"The name isn't uncommon," I said. "And I grew up in Leeuwarden, not Amsterdam—you did say she was married and living in Amsterdam, right?—right. So just give it up. If you won't accept my certainty she isn't the same person, then I can't accept yours that she is."

I watched as he added some sugar to his coffee and stirred it deliberately, his spoon dancing slow arcs and circles.

"You're right, Wim. Neither of us can be sure. Eric told me she will perform again tomorrow night, or rather, tonight. He says he can get us both an invitation so—"

"Certainly not."

He raised his hand before my protest went further. "I know. But it might be worthwhile to make sure the dancer is not someone you remembered, don't you think? And if the idea of going offends you, this is what I'll do. I'll go in your place and ask her myself. Discretely, of course. In the meantime, you can explore the Eiffel Tower or take an evening Seine cruise. Afterward, I'll let you know what I found out, and then you can leave Paris knowing one way or the other."

His reasonable-sounding proposal, given in his amiable, rational voice didn't fool me one bit. His motives were more prurient than investigative. I shook my head.

"But this way there'll be no doubts," he said.

"I have no doubts," I lied. There were doubts aplenty, along with a pressing desire to know for certain, which I struggled to restrain. "I was mistaken," I went on. "It wasn't her, couldn't be, and you would be doing me a personal favour if, like me, you chose to drop the matter altogether. I'm tired and I intend to return to Amsterdam to see my wife and child."

"Cornelia would understand if you decided to stay longer."

This was something I could not deny, just as I had to concede the possibility of Max's earlier assertion, that Cornelia might have appreciated such a show from an artistic standpoint. All the more reason, in my mind, to bury this event.

"Max, not a word about any of this to her. Or to her parents, or anyone for that matter. I have a reputation to uphold."

"Yes, I understand how my sister can get so jealous—oh, don't look at me that way. Very well, it's not as if I've never kept secrets from

Cornelia. But what will I say we did during your visit?"

"I don't know. Walked around, had dinner, walked around some more."

"The dullness will disappoint her."

"Well, better disappointed than ashamed."

"Oh Wim, you really are too much."

All the first-class compartments on the train to Amsterdam were booked. I did not look forward to several hours of mingling with the noisier, less cultured passengers in second-class. But luck was with me in the form of a near empty car at the rear of the train. I found enough space to review the contracts and papers from Marseille at leisure, with the bonus of having saved a few francs.

The train steamed northward, chugging past charming pastorals of flat farmland and green pastures cut by irrigation canals and the odd forest. My mood improved as the distance from Paris increased. With each mile it became easier to put Max, Maggie, and Mata Hari out of mind and look forward to seeing Cornelia and Antje.

Then came a long stop somewhere between Amiens and Lille where a large number of passengers boarded. By the time the train began rolling again, I was sharing my compartment with a woman who, judging by her smart attire, had also fallen victim to a lack of first-class seating. A black, silk veil obscured her face, save for a pointed, alluring chin. I wondered if she was in mourning. She took out a thin silver container from her purse and gestured for my permission to smoke.

"By all means," I said, choosing neutral English.

"Thank you," she said, answering with a British accent.

"Not at all," I said, but the smell became distracting and inhibited my concentration on one of the contracts. I set it down.

"Are you going as far as Amsterdam?" I said.

She paused, as if uncertain whether to engage me in conversation. After a long draw from her cigarette that resulted in a narrow stream of smoke upward, she turned her glance away from me to stare out the window at a large field dotted with bales of hay.

"No, to Calais."

"And what is in Calais, may I ask?"

"Nothing whatsoever."

I chuckled at her drollness. I doubted she'd intended to be entertaining, as my reaction made her frown. Our eyes fixed briefly, until she looked up sharply, letting out another mouthful of smoke.

"If you must know, sir, I am going to Calais to board a ship to London where I will meet my *husband* to catch a train to Glasgow."

Ah, she suspects me of dishonourable intentions, I thought, and the idea amused me. Perhaps my recent proximity to Max had rubbed some of his persona off on me. I made sure to display my right hand prominently, with its wedding band. Her veil lifted slightly, as if propped up by her forehead and eyebrows, revealing a pair of wine-red lips.

"You know, I've never been to London," I said.

"I prefer Paris," she said, evenly, her mouth twitching. Her veil made it impossible to tell if it was a smile or a smirk.

"It seems many women do," I said, unable to hold back a slight sneer.

"Every true woman ought to," she said, her tone matching mine.

Touché, I thought, and left it at that.

She disembarked at Lille to catch her connection for Calais, leaving me alone in the compartment, except for a lingering plume of smoke from her doused cigarette. I again had difficulty concentrating on my work, this time due to a hunger that grew when forced to wait for the aisle-clogging passport inspection. I then endured another long line to negotiate the food car, the first real inconvenience of travelling in the lower class. But it was worth the trouble. It seemed so long since I had tasted pure Dutch milk and enjoyed spiced Gouda cheese on a sandwich, with ham. The bread so fresh. Practical as they might be, no baguette could ever satisfy me so well.

For a good hour I was able to get back to my work obligations The more I realized what my father-in-law and I accomplished in Marseille, the happier I became. The van Rozebout firm could expect very large profits this year. But with that, naturally, would come a great deal of administrative work. That meant hiring more staff, which would not be easy; there seemed such a dearth of reliable and capable young men available.

I had been tempted, while in Paris, to recruit Max to help us out, which he'd done in the past from time to time for brief periods, whenever his father really needed him. Max understood the business well enough but his focus and work habits left much to be desired, so his involvement was always a mixed blessing. Mr. van Rozebout's lifelong dream of his only son inheriting the business vanished years before when Max abruptly announced one day he was going to travel the world. It was obvious his desire was to escape such a destiny but all he managed was to get to Africa; he was back in a month. The lingering shame from this episode ensured Max would answer the call whenever urgently needed. For my part, I had little use for him in any capacity. Still, in impending staff shortages, he was better than no one. Then again, after the previous night, who knew?

The winter frost was receding and tall green grass spilled out of the trackside ditches that kept grazing horses, cows, and sheep from straying. An occasional heron, brightly coloured tulip field, or village distinguished by a single church steeple, broke up the monotony of this flatter land. I set aside my documents and leaned my shoulder into the window.

A small family interrupted my dozing. Such a racket their bustling made as they took off their coats and filled the upper racks with battered luggage. Two children, a boy and a girl who might have been twins around six years old, sat across from me, beside their father, while their mother took the place next to mine. The man doffed his hat and volunteered a friendly smile, which I returned. Then he motioned for his children to look out the window, pointed at a farm that stood in front of a village, and spoke with a thin but firm Rotterdam accent.

"Look quick, Hans, Sophie, see all the animals. See how that church steeple seems to come out of the barn."

The children harmonized an agreeable cooing sound before becoming silent. Then, with no presumption, the boy asked his mother for a *dropje*. Dear little Sophie joined her brother in looking up hopefully at their mother. She was not an attractive woman—although I suspected she once was—but her smile exuded warmth and pride, kindness and benevolence. Raising these two adorable children had earned the woman her maternal badge of honour, her stoutness and greyish, stern face. The obvious love for her family touched me.

I looked away as she dug into her handbag to ensure she would feel no obligation to offer me one. Quietly, the children chewed on the salted liquorice, alternating between joining their father looking out the window and glancing curiously at my papers, their faces squinting from the sour treat. I was particularly enamoured with Sophie, who had a tiny dimple on her cheek similar to Antje's. Would my daughter turn out as polite as this cherub?

The question troubled me for I was not confident of a positive answer. Barely more than a year old, Antje was already showing signs of her mother's lesser traits. Most notably her impudence, punctuated by an embarrassing habit of pinching people, particularly those she met for the first time. Most, including Cornelia, found it amusing. I did not.

A light but persistent drizzle, accompanied by a fog and dark clouds, filled the view out the window, making it impossible to read the signpost of the village where the little family exited. I smiled polite farewells to Hans and Sophie and their parents. The children giggled and hesitated, even looked as if they might sit back down, until their father gently squeezed their necks to push them forward. The drizzle turned to diagonal rain, which pelted at the windows as if demanding entry.

The family's absence left a dreary emptiness in the compartment. I shut my eyes but instead of sleep, my mind tormented me with mixed images of Mata Hari dancing on the stage in Paris and of spending time with Maggie by our tree at the Grote Kerk in Leeuwarden. I tried to discern anything that might eliminate the possibility my old friend and the dancer were the same person. That led to second-guessing my hasty departure from Paris. Now I wished I had somehow confirmed whether I'd been right or wrong about her identity. Yet turning back would be an absurd waste of time and money.

At Amsterdam's Centraal Station, the conductor nudged me awake with an impatient push and addressed me with an insolent voice.

"Sir, you must exit the train."

I was about to berate him for his lack of respect but then recalled I was in second-class, and that I should not be surprised to be treated as such.

"What's the rush?" I asked politely. "The train terminates here, doesn't it?"

"Actually, sir, this train will continue north, to Leeuwarden."

"To Leeuwarden, you say?" I said. A crow in a windless sky, I calculated, could fly the sixty miles straight north over the Zuiderzee to the Frisian capital. The train, on the other hand, would have to travel east via Zwolle to bypass that offshoot of the North Sea, adding half the distance again to the bird's most efficient route, resulting in another four to five hours on the train and a late evening arrival. The temptation to return to the place where I had known Maggie was strong. I could have gone too because Cornelia had expected me to stay longer with Max. But my desire to return to my family won out.

"Sir, please, unless you pay the extra fare, I must ask that you exit immediately."

"Of course," I said, but waved away his offer to call for a porter, choosing instead to manage my own luggage.

A surge of energy uplifted me as soon as I disembarked. It helped that it was no longer raining. Having taken an earlier train than originally planned, I had time to walk home and, on the way, shop for a gift for Antje. I enlisted a porter after all and arranged to have my bags sent home ahead of me.

I exited Centraal Station onto the wide Damrak but then made my way into the narrower, shadier Nieuwendijk. Avoiding the rain puddles made navigating the throng of pedestrian traffic cumbersome. Worse, nothing satisfactory presented itself in the shops. I crossed Dam square, passing the Royal Palace, into Kalverstraat. I soon regretted this. Between noon and four o'clock, by some unofficial custom or covenant, women of a certain type and the men who wanted to meet them overtook the Kalverstraat. The best shops were here, though, including a couple of fine toy stores and general stores with large toy departments. I kept my head down as I walked in order to repel solicitations.

Finally, in the far back of a toy shop, I found a soft, knitted giraffe. Antje loved the giraffes at Artis Zoo best of all. This one was a poor replica of the real thing but I was confident my daughter would still recognize and enjoy it. I came out of the Kalverstraat at the Muntplein, crossed the busy intersection, and stopped at the floating flower market where I purchased a dozen red roses for Cornelia.

My arms filled with gifts, my heart filled with good feeling, I escaped to the other side of the Amstel where, thankfully, there were fewer people. Their numbers dwindled further the closer I got to the Herengracht. The sun glanced on a pair of cats lazing next to each other on a houseboat in front of our house. They paid no attention to me as I walked up our steps.

I gave my coat to my manservant, Vincent, and found Cornelia and Antje in the rear sitting room. The green room. This was Cornelia's favourite because it looked out on the garden and because its olive-green walls held a host of family portraits, all painted with the same dark, forest-green backgrounds. Some dated back to the seventeenth century. Even with the gold trim on the doors and wainscoting, the room was too stifling, too van Rozebout.

"Oh, hello there," Cornelia said, struggling to put on Antje's coat. My wife's face brightened when I showed her the roses. "Are those for me?"

I proffered the flowers in exchange for my daughter. Cornelia resisted, holding on to Antje, motioning for me to let them through.

"Where are you going?" I said.

"I'm taking Antje to the doctor."

"Is something wrong?" I said, at the same time touching my daughter's forehead, which was warm but not overly warm.

"Nothing's wrong, only routine."

"But it's so late in the day," I said. "Leave it till tomorrow. I have a gift for her."

"Ugh, not another toy. You've got to stop buying them for her."

"It's hard."

"I know but just keep it hidden for now, all right? Otherwise I'll never get her out. I'm already an hour late for our appointment with Dr. Sluiter."

"Doctor who?"

"He's new. We won't be long."

"What happened to Dr. Neeskens?"

"Nothing happened to Dr. Neeskens. Antje just prefers Dr. Sluiter."

"Why wasn't I consulted?"

"Oh Wim, I don't have time to explain now."

With that, they left me. I gave the flowers to Cornelia's servant, Madeline. I was about to sit in the big armchair but then saw Antje's toys, all of which I'd bought for her, the letter blocks, colourful clown top, and a doll strewn about the floor. Irked, I called Madeline back to tidy the mess, and then to get Vincent to make me some tea and bring it to the canal-side room.

This was my sanctuary. The powder blue diamond-patterned wallpaper blended well with the ornate Turkish rug of deep blues, greys, and yellows. Whilst sitting in the oversized, modern wingback chair, one could appreciate the pastoral paintings of the Dutch countryside and at the same time observe the goings-on outside by the waterway.

The tea came. I drank it impatiently, and so scalding the roof of my mouth. For some reason, I began staring at two paintings hanging above a bookshelf, each showing a transatlantic steamers navigating the port in Rotterdam, one arriving, one departing. Their dreamy ochre colouring gave me a sense of melancholy.

My attention then drifted to the writing table below the paintings, strewn with mail accumulated during my absence.

It was all the usual correspondence except for a lemon-coloured envelope. It looked like a party invitation, except then Cornelia would have opened it. The Leeuwarden return address, penned in small, swirling letters, each line perfectly horizontal, startled me. The envelope contained a note on a white card, a single paragraph rather tersely announcing the passing of my uncle, Dick Terpstra, last week. An instinctual feeling of sadness came over me but didn't last long. It had been years since I last had contact with my relatives in Friesland.

Cornelia and Antje returned a couple of hours later. I took my daughter, and held her up above me to where she could see everything in the room like a bird. A quick descent usually rewarded me with a neck hug. Instead, she yawned before her head drooped against my shoulder. It seemed pointless to give her the toy now.

"I thought you said you wouldn't be long," I said, not concealing my frustration. Cornelia was looking away and missed my tone, or she ignored it.

"Such a lovely day, I took a longer route. Of course, stopped the Dam to feed the pigeons."

"Of course," I said. "But you know I had been hoping to take her for a walk while it was still light out."

"Oh, Wim, I'm sorry. But summer's coming. There'll be plenty of other chances. And just look at her tired smile. You can tell she had a nice time, and I did too. Now she should have no trouble getting to sleep."

"I suppose," I said.

She took my daughter from me to take her upstairs. Antje was usually resistant to leaving my arms, but not this time. That bothered me.

Cornelia came back and took a seat on the divan. She seemed in a good mood and I decided not to concern myself with the switch in doctors. I was about to pass her the letter but before I could, she called for Madeline to bring us two new steaming cups of tea and a plate of fresh *gebakjes*, from her favourite pastry shop, which she had taken the time to purchase on her way home.

"So, tell me about your adventures in France," she said, as she took the seat opposite me.

"All terrific," I smiled. "Our business could increase by nearly fifteen percent this year, and more beyond."

"No, not that. How was your time with my brother? Did he entertain you well?"

The tea came then, thankfully, and I began to wonder if Cornelia knew something about the Guimet; even that she may have put Max up to it.

"Have you talked to your brother?"

"Now how or when could I have talked to my brother?"

I shrugged and helped myself to one of the smaller *gebakjes*, which I ingested whole, only to give me more time to consider my response. Cornelia gave me a hard stare.

"You have such boorish manners, sometimes, you know," she said. "As if you still think you're living in that little town up north."

"Speaking of which," I said, swallowing the last piece and then wiping my mouth with an exaggeratedly dainty motion. "Sad news while I was away."

I handed her the card. Cornelia took a long time reading it, perhaps unsure how to react. Patiently, I sipped my tea, until finally she put it down.

"I think we ought to pay respects, in person," I said.

She paused first for two drawn out sips before saying, "But the service was last week."

"I realize that."

"Surely, you don't intend for us to rush all the way up to Friesland? I don't mean any disrespect, Wim, but well, I've never met these people. And you haven't had contact with them since you were a child. Do you even remember them?"

My wife was right about my lack of contact with the Terpstras. I now wondered how they'd found my address. But they had, which meant they had made an effort, which meant I now felt an obligation to go. Whether I would have been of the same mind had I not encountered Maggie in Paris was debatable. Cornelia nibbled idly on another pastry, although I sensed her watching me.

"They're the only family I have left."

"What about your work? You've already been gone a week."

"Cornelia, since when are you so worried about matters at the office?"

"I'm just afraid you'll come back to find it all a mess. Then I'll have to suffer your brooding about the laziness and complacence of young workers today."

Again, she had a point, even if articulated in such an inelegant way. But I doubted one more day would make much difference.

"I'll be back home tomorrow night."

"Well Antje and I will stay in Amsterdam."

"That's fine," I said. "I understand."

She gave me a funny look, as if unsure about something. I didn't dare ask lest she discern my other motive for going. Or worse, that she would change her mind and come along.

Maggie

So how was it possible for a young girl, raised in the calm and placid environment of a town like Leeuwarden, to come to dance so disgracefully in raucous Paris? It didn't seem possible and that's what I kept telling myself during the long train ride, although never to the point of being convinced. On the other hand, if Maggie indeed was Mata Hari, I would want to know. Perhaps do something about it. With a young daughter of my own, I would be a negligent father if I failed to do that much for my parental peer. Of course, I truly intended to pay respects to my uncle too, even though that was not uppermost in my mind upon arrival.

I emerged from the station into wet streets but dry skies, a blustery wind pushing the clouds away. Trees swayed as citizens clutched the thick lapels of their buttoned-up coats. The cabmen, dutifully lined up alongside their horses, seemed oblivious to the North Sea chill. None expressed interest in this potential client so I strolled past them toward the town center. I preferred to walk anyway and keep my business to myself.

I managed just a few steps when a bicycle almost hit me. In avoiding it, my posterior hit the backside of a horse that barely moved but whinnied in response. The bicycle rider, instead of cursing me, as his counterpart in Paris no doubt would have, helped me to my feet and apologized. He then kindly directed me north across the canal that circled the city to a wide and familiar shopping avenue divided by another canal.

Storeowners were drawing up awnings, creating a harmonic clattering of commercial optimism. Several proprietors swept doorways while others moved racks of wares out into the street, interrupting their tasks for brief greetings to passers-by. There were no children around; they would be in school, of course. A few crows perched on a telegraph wire near the bakery, scanned the scene below for specks of food. With each step I took, the sense of belonging increased, along with a stronger sense of orientation, but a conspicuous absence of nostalgia.

A short walk along the encircling canal brought me to the Willemskade. Now I felt more at home; it seemed so unchanged from the Willemskade when my father and I had lived here. Houseboats hugged both sides of the canal. Their black hulls jostled in the wake of other vessels, narrowing the waterway until it curved into an intersection with the western side canal and another that went beyond the city. The street and its tight row of plain two-

and three-storey houses curved along its edge. Subtle yet persistent odours of boiled cabbage, dank canal water, and manure reminded me of those days too.

A commotion drew my attention, coming from an animated crowd near the water's edge. A mother and her young daughter were sitting on the ground in front of an overturned fruit crate. I stopped to observe as the mother lifted the crate, revealing an ersatz corral for several kittens. She brusquely held back the other felines while grabbing a black-and-white tabby by its scruff. She handed it to a greedy child whose mother gave back some coins in return. Meanwhile, the seller's daughter kept wiping tears from her eyes.

"Enough of your crying, child. It's off to a better home."

"I know," said the girl, through her sobs.

The scene filled me with gloom; I wished I'd ignored it and gone straight to the house of apartments where Maggie lived the last time I saw her. Now, about to knock, my hand froze. What was I doing here? I had never dared knock on this door when I lived here fifteen years before; what logic would impel me to do so now? Furthermore, what business was it of mine what Margaretha Zelle did today, or at any time in her life?

But her family was my concern. They might be unaware of what their daughter, or sister, was up to. In their place, I reminded myself, I'd want to know. A small, yawning old man answered my knock.

"I'm looking for Mr. Zelle," I said.

"And you are?"

"An old family friend."

The odd fellow regarded me with suspicion but seemed unable to determine who or what I was, and so remained mute.

"What about Margaretha Zelle?" I said.

"Haven't lived here for at least ten years."

He shut the door on me then. He didn't slam it, didn't curse at me, he simply shut the door as if I had become invisible. Now what? I wondered, as I resumed walking along the canal, trying to ignore the mewing of the two or three kittens not yet spoken for.

This abrupt termination of my quest was not something I had expected. But what had I expected? To find someone from Maggie's family still here, ideally Maggie herself, married to someone—even Bart Postma—and living a relatively prosperous life? Maybe not, but surely a forwarding address, or some clue as to what happened to her or her family. Not a dead end.

It was still too early in the day to surprise my relatives—for undoubtedly my visit would come as a surprise to them—so I took a leisurely stroll along Leeuwarden's quiet streets, not mindful of where I was going.

Eventually, my footsteps took me to the *Grote of Jacobijnerkerk*, or Great Church. Erected in the thirteenth century, this red-bricked jumble of contours, triangular gables and roofs dominated its environs. A series of narrow, cobbled streets of modest brick houses fanned out asymmetrically in several directions. I recalled, with ironic amusement, my initial aversion to this place and to church in general.

Oh, the excuses I would come up with to avoid going, the tantrums when they failed. I was such an incorrigible boy then. My father had such enduring patience, a quiet passivity that I took advantage of with tactics that worked six days a week. Yet I could never win when it came to the Sabbath. Somehow—to this day, I still cannot remember how—my father would rouse me out of bed, wait out my protests, and manage to get me into my best clothes. Once in those clothes something would change in me to make me behave, at least for a few hours. We would join the congregating citizens from all parts of town, occasionally pausing to converse with some—I would keep morosely quiet—until we reached the heavy wooden doors opened wide to sweep us in. A slow-moving hour of singing, praying, and listening while sitting on a hard pew. It always seemed longer. During this time, I would imagine my sins—every single, slightest one—exposed by an invisible beam shooting from the steeple. What an ordeal.

When the service ended, I felt as if freed from bondage. While my father talked with people afterward, I would hasten to a lonely tree that stood in a small, hedge-bordered grassy square, beyond which a small archway led to an annex of tiny houses. I would race there like an explorer claiming it for his monarch, and then wait impatiently for my father to come and get me, brooding over the fact the cycle would repeat the following Sunday.

What a difficult youth I must have been at eleven, I thought with some shame and regret, as I wandered around looking for that tree. And there it was. It had grown in all these years yet seemed smaller now. Of course, I was much taller too. Perspectives and natural things change and develop in their own proportions. Just as my attitude did beginning one particular summer Sunday in 1888.

With the trees and flowers in full bloom that day, the freshness of spring still in my spirits, my breath stopped when I exited the church doors and saw a girl standing in my spot, a girl I had never seen before in my life. She was wearing a pink dress and a purple flower in her hair. Her arms were crossed and her body leaned listlessly at an awkward angle against my tree, the grandeur of which her presence easily upstaged.

I approached nonchalantly to get a closer look at her before arousing attention. She had an unusually dark and long face, narrow nose, with slightly jutting chin and small lower lip, so unique in this town of blonde, pale-skinned, blue-eyed girls.

"Hello," I said, a crack in my voice.

She raised herself and, as she was taller than most girls and many boys too, she seemed pleasantly surprised to have to look up at me.

"Hello," she said.

"How are you?"

"Bored."

"Me too," I said.

"You have a funny accent."

"So do you."

She chuckled and then grabbed at a bright green leaf, tenderly stroking it before using it to cover her smile. Then she said something in French, a language I was only beginning to learn then. The way she said it, as if we already knew each other, as if we were continuing a broken-off conversation, thrilled me.

"Can you translate that?" I said.

"Of course."

And she did. Not in Dutch, but in German, or at least I thought it was German. Then she laughed and kept laughing until she had me nearly begging her to repeat it in Dutch. It was something silly like, "My birthday is soon. Should I ask daddy for a new purse, or a new dress, or both?"

I then translated those words into American English, putting as much Mark Twain vernacular as a Manhattan native could muster. We both laughed at that for several minutes.

"So what's my name in English?" she said.

"What's your name in Dutch?"

She gave me an odd look, as if affronted that I, or anyone for that matter, would not know who she was.

"Margaretha Geertruida."

I paused for a moment, only for effect though, to make it seem I had to think about it.

"Margaret Gertrude," I said.

"That's not much different," she said, frowning. "At least here, people can call me M'Greet, Gresha, Griet. Can't you do better?"

I took longer this time, anxious to impress her with something unique, something that would prolong the conversation. Nothing came to me until I caught her eyes straying and realized that any second she could walk away.

"Maggie," I said.

Her mouth twitched in delight as she repeated the name, replacing the soft English double consonant with the hard Dutch one in variations that translated it into magic and words about the stomach and stomach pains. I told her we could meet again next week to work on it.

"And who are you?" she said.

"Wim Brink."

"But that's a Dutch name," she said. "I thought you were American."

"I am American. I was born in New York."

"New *Amsterdam*," she said, grinning.

"New *York*," I said.

"Never mind," she said, and then grabbed my hand and pulled me away.

"What are you doing?" I said, trying to conceal my panic.

"Please. How can an American be so timid? Besides, you're not alone, you're with me."

Those words, "you're with me," swept me along. I followed her to Grote Kerkstraat, a curving street of elegant homes. Maggie then released my hand and pushed me along Kleine Hoogstraat. We stopped when we came upon a square so she could point out her private school. She then guided us along Grote Hoogstraat until we reached the Kelders and its canal-side rows of shops and narrow houses of varying heights and fancy gables. We strolled to the middle of the bridge over the canal where we stopped to look over the rail.

"Tell me, Wim Brink, do people in America really name their children, Maggie?" This time she'd enunciated the name perfectly; it made me feel foolish. She laughed at my dismay. "Well, do they?"

"Actually, it's a familiar name for Margaret, in America."

"Maggie, Margaret, Maggie, Margaret. I like that. It can be your special name for me."

I blushed at the notion of a proprietary link to this wonderful girl and vowed, to myself, to call her Maggie from then on. And to forcefully deal with anyone else who dared to do the same.

Then she pointed to a shop with a freshly painted green doorway between two windows displaying a variety of men's hats on pegs: bowlers, top hats, beret, porkpies, and more. A sign above each glass pane read A. Zelle.

"My father owns that store . . . and plenty of others too," she said, although losing some of the certainty in her voice.

"Is that so?" I said.

"Yes, that's so."

"My father bought a hat from your father once," I said. I remembered that day well, too, because my father—the calmest man I'd ever met—had exchanged strong words with the man behind the counter about the price. I refrained from mentioning that.

"Do you live above the store?" I said.

She gave me an unkind look, as if insulted. Then she grinned and pointed far down the right hand side of the canal to a row of shops. Behind them stood the magnificent gothic spire of Saint Boniface church towering over the city.

"That's where I live."

"In one of the shops in front of the church?"

"No."

"Don't tell me you live in the church?"

"Stop it, Wim Brink. Look straight ahead."

The only possibility left was Caminghastate, the most famous landmark in Leeuwarden, a grand three-storey mansion with majestic pillars, crowned by a small but ornate gable adorned with a coat of arms. The curving lines of the gable fell like a girl's braided hair.

Most certainly she had to be lying, but I could not determine whether she had made it up for a joke, hoping I would play along, or because she really wanted me to believe her.

"You must be wealthy then," I said.

"Of course."

"With lots of servants?"

"Lots of servants."

"So many servants that some of them even have their own servants?" I said.

"You laugh but I'll have you know several are dedicated only to me."

"Oh? How come they're not with you now?"

Maggie's face changed; my response, rather than spurring her on, disappointed her.

"Okay, you can stop now, I know you're making this all up," I said.

She shoved me playfully and everything seemed all right again.

"If you must know, we did live above the store once, but now we own a very nice house on Grote Kerkstraat."

That was a fine address too, and certainly elegant and affluent enough for any boaster I knew. It was strange, though, because we had just walked down that same street a few minutes earlier and she'd shown no sign indicating we'd passed her house. Still, I chose to believe her, partly because I wanted to—it was on the way to church and trying to spot her would be a pleasant weekly distraction—and partly because I feared if I challenged one more claim she might run off and I'd never see her again.

"I should return to my father," I said. And then, with my heart beating faster, my voice shaking, I added, "Come with me. Then I'll walk you home."

"No, my daddy promised to take me for a drive, and I'm supposed to wait for him by the store."

"Will you meet me again? At the tree?"

"Why not?" she said, with a shrug.

Not the unequivocal affirmation I wanted but better than a refusal.

An agonizing six days ensued, during which I replayed our conversation in my mind. Every word, every gesture, dozens of times a day.

She did show up the following week, and subsequent weeks, sometimes content to stay and talk by the tree, other times wishing to wander. I began to look forward to Sundays, and to church, which confused my father but pleased him too. Yet I never ran into her in Grote Kerkstraat, where she supposedly lived, or anywhere else in town for that matter.

With Maggie dominating my thoughts, the few friends I had quickly lost my interest. Consequently, I got into fewer fights, although the ones I did get into grew more violent. My attention became absorbed by Sundays, the one that had just passed as much as the one to come. My special and private torment, the anticipation of spending up to half an hour with this delightful girl countered by the fear that she could stop showing at any time. The odd thing was that, while the six days leading up to Sunday were torturous, a calm patience came over me in church. I even began to enjoy the sermons, to listen to them, to try to understand the message, cherishing that last hour of anticipation.

Then, after the final hymn and the final amen, I would meet Maggie by the tree. Usually I was there first but sometimes—and those were the best moments—she was waiting for me. In her clear, pleasant voice, she would tell me about school, how she did well in French and German and writing poetry, but also that she struggled with Needlework and Singing and Gymnastics; how the teachers often reproached her behaviour in class; how popular she was in spite of the envy over the bright and colourful dresses her father bought and let her wear to school.

As for her home life, Maggie complained about her three younger brothers but spoke seldom about her mother. Most of all, she enjoyed bragging about her father, about his accomplishments and how he spoiled her. For her sixth birthday, so she claimed, Mr. Zelle bought her a *bokkenwagen*, a goat carriage, to transport her around town. She proved it with a photograph of herself, sitting in a small carriage on the road, two white goats standing proudly, waiting for the whip's command, while her family observed from the sidewalk.

"I guess you live in Caminghastate after all," I said.

She rewarded this with a generous smile. Then she showed me another photograph of a painting of a bearded man in white trousers and a top hat. He was sitting on a horse, regally holding the Leeuwarden coat of arms.

"That's my father. He had it commissioned when he was selected as a standard bearer for the Guard of Honour to greet King Willem."

Impressed as I was, I began to notice these family anecdotes all occurred years before. Unless she was making something up or talking about school, and aside from her personal successes and petty complaints, she avoided the present.

Anyone who paid attention to the gossip in the neighbourhood—as I began to—learned Mr. Zelle had gone bankrupt that winter. In general, he was a capable businessman, evidenced by his successful hat shop and profitable stock market speculating. But he went too far and lost all he had, including his haberdashery. He garnered little sympathy within the town. Many people considered Adam Zelle vain, arrogant, pompous, and pretentious. My father described him once as a man with a big city ego trapped in a small town, or something along those lines, the closest thing to an insult I ever heard from my kind-hearted dad. It seemed best not to bring any of this up with Maggie on Sundays, though. By now I had seen enough sides of her personality to know her moods could turn on a single mistimed remark.

Then one hot Sunday the following summer, not caring about getting dirt on her lacy white dress, she showed up and sat on the ground, her sad face drooped in her hands. We'd been meeting for about a year and I'd never seen her this way before. When I kneeled down and asked what was wrong, she accidentally rubbed her fingers across my bare knee.

"We have to move," she said.

"Oh?" I said, alarmed. Distracted by her touch, I shifted my position until she removed her hand. "Where?"

"My daddy's going to The Hague, to find work," she said, with pitiful sadness.

"You're going to the Hague?"

"I didn't say that."

"Where are you moving to then?" I said.

She shrugged as if she didn't know, or didn't care, but when I pressed her, she told me the address on the Willemskade. I almost jumped from joy and would have if she hadn't been so glum.

"What are you grinning about?" she said.

"That's just around the corner from my house."

"It's where poor people live."

"We're not poor," I said, no longer smiling, but still happy inside.

Her words got lost in my daydreams. Not only about us walking to and from church on Sundays but also spending time together during the week. I imagined ways to persuade her to come over for dinner.

Alas, things did not turn out as I hoped. While she still kept our Sunday appointments, the quantity of our Sabbath time together actually decreased. Whenever I suggested she stay longer and walk home with me, offering my father as chaperone, she smiled as if interested, but always declined, promising she'd think about it the following week. She also had gotten to know a few more boys and now I had to share my Sunday time with them. Those rare winks and touches on the arms I used to treasure lost their value the first time her fingers brushed the arm of a rival.

One Sunday, after a maddeningly long sermon, knowing we would have less time together than usual, I rushed to our tree, and waited. I was happy to find no other boys there and I looked forward to being alone with Maggie.

People streamed out from the large doors into the streets, gathering into small groups, but there was no sign of her. Nearly ten frustrating minutes went by before I glimpsed a bright dress only one person could wear. But she was not alone. She was with Bart Postma, a schoolmate of mine, over at the far end of the hedged-in lawn, giggling. Not only did it become obvious Maggie was not going to join me at the tree, she was going to allow Bart to escort her home.

I didn't know what to do. In those paralyzing seconds of indecision, an impulsive fury took hold of me. I heard my father call my name but I ignored him and instead ran off to follow Maggie and Bart. I caught up at the end of the road and squeezed in between them, just before their arms or shoulders could touch.

"Oh Wim, there you are," Maggie said, offhandedly.

I gently nudged her aside and shoved Bart several times. The way he laughed at me, he probably thought I was playing, or clumsy. I hated him for his lack of comprehension almost as much as for being with Maggie. But he was of no significance.

"Why weren't you at the tree?" I said.

"Bart wanted to show me something."

"Show you what, Maggie?"

"Show you what, Maggie?" Bart repeated, mocking me.

Bart was a good kid, though, and I knew his taunting wasn't mean-spirited, but that made no difference. I threw him down to the ground, jumped on him, and began punching. Poor Bart tried to punch back but I had position on him and several of my punches connected with his face before he could put up his hands.

"Wim, what are you doing? Stop it. He's bleeding."

"I don't care," I said, prying his hands apart to get at his face.

"You're hurting him."

That's right, I thought at that moment, and I wanted to hurt him too. And make him cry. But then Maggie let out a pitiful gasp, which affected me more than any verbal plea could have. I stopped and stood up, placing one foot on Bart's chest. He remained lying down, whimpering but not crying, touching his bloody nose, which, fortunately, had not broken.

"You can leave us now, Wim," Maggie said.

The regal inflection in her voice suggested to me her anger was not absolute, that part of her appreciated what I'd done as an expression of passion. The way a discerning queen might elect to see noble motivation behind the oafish act of one of her subjects. As long as I respected her wish and left immediately, our friendship would remain intact.

That assumption proved inaccurate and I spent the next three miserable Sundays alone by the tree, never even spotting her. In the neighbourhood, whenever she saw me, she turned the other way. Each time it happened, it hurt, and I began to take my pain out on my schoolmates as I regressed into former habits. My poor dad could do little, my teachers not much more. However, I still behaved one day out of seven a week, just in case.

On the fourth Maggie-less Sunday, the church held a special service to honour local men who had died fighting in the East Indies. Those who owned a military uniform, whether used in the East Indies or not, were encouraged to wear it to service. That was the first time I ever saw my father in his Zouave uniform.

I couldn't imagine how anyone could have fought with any effectiveness in that button-less short jacket, which barely fit around my father's now stout frame, with its broad and long sash. Unlike the prim red or blue coats with gold or silver epaulettes that others wore, my father's uniform was plain and of a greenish colour. The baggy trousers and white leggings were more practical. At the calf, a short leather cuff stood out, which according to my father was called a *jambiere*. A grand fez, a red folded hat with a yellow tassel, completed the ensemble. His unit—the 5th New York Infantry Regiment, often referred to as Duryée's Zouaves for their leader, Colonel Abram Duryée—wore this fighting for the Unionists in the American Civil War. It looked ridiculous to me, comical even, and I dreaded showing up at church next to my father. I began concocting new excuses to stay home that Sunday.

I had a few ready but forgot them when I spotted what looked like a bloodstain on the re-sewn shoulder. I looked further and found four other blemishes. All of them—the shoulder one a gunshot wound and the others knife wounds—had come in 1862 at the Second Battle of Manassas, also known as Bull Run, a fierce fight in which many of my father's fellow Duryées died. I knew my father had participated in battles, only he rarely mentioned them, and I never inquired. Hence, all my knowledge of the Civil War came from my history lessons in New York, to which I had paid scant attention. Intrigued by the wounds, I made him tell me more, specifically how many he'd wounded or killed himself. He declined to answer that question but did offer many stories about his experiences training in New York and fighting in Virginia. My interest grew with every word as my abashed indifference turned to pride. That day I saw my father far differently than I ever had before.

After church, I ignored the tree to stand proudly next to my dad while he talked with many people, including several who normally would not speak with him otherwise.

"How unique," Maggie said behind me, her voice one I'd recognize anywhere, anytime. I turned to see her smiling, nodding toward my father. I tried to act aloof and struggled to keep a smile from bursting out. "And I love that hat."

"It's a fez," I said.

She ignored my tone and stared, as if waiting for me to tell her more. My face blushed under her gaze; I was not accustomed to having centre stage in her presence.

"My dad was a Zouave, in the American Civil War."

"Zouave?" she said. "Those are French, aren't they, from North Africa?"

"I don't know anything about that. My dad's unit was based in New York. They fought mostly in Virginia."

When she touched my arm, my skin filled with goose bumps.

"You should be like your father and become a soldier, or better yet, an officer," she said.

"I don't know," I said.

"Was your father an officer?" she said.

"No."

"Well, that's all right, I suppose. Anyway, he looks quite handsome dressed like that. You would too."

"In that uniform?"

"Well, yes, you would look fine in that. But I imagine you could do much better if you began early so you could become an officer. Yes, I think a military career is right for you. After all, you already know how to fight and draw blood."

She had said it with the most delicate trace of sarcasm.

"Are you still mad at me?" I said.

"If you say you're sorry to Bart Postma, we can be friends again."

"Where is he?"

"He went home when I told him I was coming over to see you."

I paused to give my heart a chance to slow down.

"First thing tomorrow, at school," I said. "Promise."

"*Bien*. Now why don't you accompany me home?"

I offered my arm. To my delight, she took it, and we began walking off. I wanted to tell my father, who was saying goodbye to some other people, but was too afraid to let go. However, we only went a few steps before Maggie stopped abruptly.

"We should wait for your father."

"What for?"

"I insist."

After I introduced them, I purposely slowed our pace to let my father get ahead. She didn't seem to notice or mind; something else was in her thoughts. She paused at a fine house, which I guessed to be her former residence.

"My daddy's coming back from The Hague next week," she said, as we continued walking.

"That's nice," I said.

"Nice? It's more than nice. It means we'll get to live in a splendid house again, like this one."

"Are you sure?" I said, trying not to sound sceptical.

"Of course, I'm sure," Maggie said, but she wasn't looking at me.

I had already heard that Adam Zelle's endeavours in The Hague had failed. Her naivety saddened me. Even sadder, though, was that was the last time Maggie and I ever talked. Nearly two years of wonderful friendship ended when, a few days later, on the day she got back her father, I lost mine.

I was always envious of Maggie's affection for her dad. The death of mine—a horrible accident with a horse and cart that knocked him out and into the canal, where he drowned—didn't affect me as it would have Maggie. His military achievements notwithstanding, I saw my father as a weak man and never looked up to him as much as I ought to have. As I did my grandfather. Opa Geert's discipline and moral guidance were what I desperately needed at that point in my life, not my father's tolerance.

Had my father lived longer, had I stayed in Leeuwarden, who could say how my life would have turned out? Not well, though, would have been my conclusion then, in 1905. Maybe now too. Opa Geert's influence, and Oma Isabelle's too, made me the man and father I would become, as well as a man who could grasp what a cold, difficult child he had been.

I knelt by the lonely tree and said a long prayer for my dad's soul in Heaven, seeking his forgiveness, and his guidance. I did the same for Maggie too, wondering where she might be. For the idea of the woman dancing in Paris being the same girl who had meant so much to me then was impossible to conceive.

Then I remembered the Tulip Lady. That was the nickname the Willemskade kids gave Mrs. Huizenga, a widow who cleaned houses in the neighbourhood. If she was still alive, she could help me.

I hastened to retrace my steps. Wanting to avoid the kitten auction, I re-approached the Willemskade from the north, where the canal curved, with the Zelle house around the corner but out of sight. Every door and window frame in this row had been recently repainted in bright whites and greens, shades and curtains long replaced. That made it difficult to determine the specific house I was looking for, or even the one my father and I had occupied. Until I saw the wooden knocker sculpted in the shape of a tulip, polished to perfection.

I knocked once and waited about ten seconds. The woman who answered was the same grey haired, buxom, matronly woman I remembered, only older. Mrs. Huizenga was wearing a thick, navy blue dress with a cream-coloured lace collar, highlighted by a large broach of three tulips. A pleasantly nostalgic odour of vinegar and brown sugar emanated from inside her house. Her hands were dirty with soil.

"Mrs. Huizenga? Do you remember me? Wim Brink?"

The name meant something to her but my long face, which bore little resemblance to my father's, and moustache probably confused her.

"My father was Hans Brink?"

"Ah, yes, of course," she said, with a warm smile, and bid me to follow her inside.

The spotless house would make a splendid showpiece for prospective clients, assuming Mrs Huizenga still did that. Light curtains in the front room let in the maximum amount of sunshine. Countless shelves displayed oriental knickknacks and small, framed pictures of jungles and elephants. A large portrait of Major Huizenga, in full uniform astride a large black horse, overlooking a large, green field, hung on a wall. The red velvet scabbard, also depicted in the portrait, hung just above the sofa, sheathing a large bayonet. Next to it, a glass-covered case protecting about a dozen medals symmetrically arranged. The Javanese souvenirs strewn about the room reminded me of Mata Hari, but without the impure connotation.

Mrs. Huizenga led me toward the kitchen where I took a seat at a small table. One of its edges stood flush against a wall, papered in a flower pattern—not tulips, surprisingly. Above the cupboards, a row of matching Delft dinner plates, each with a distinct Frisian winter scene: two of canal skaters, one of a family dragging a sled across a snowy field toward a windmill, another of a small boat iced in against a shore, and two more of skaters with bent sticks chasing a small, black object.

Through a window in the back door, I could see a garden covered with dark soil, prepared to burst with new tulips in several weeks. So many tulips. All of us kids would tease each other that she'd serve them for dinner to guests. It was always a joke that whenever a boy got into trouble, we'd torment him by saying his parents were going to make him eat at Mrs. Huizenga's.

She came back from washing her hands and I gladly accepted her offer of tea for I was thirsty. The teapot, cups, and saucers Mrs. Huizenga used to serve our tea were also made of pure Delft china and, this time, with tulips painted on. A gift from my father? I was hungry too, and thrilled when she brought out a small plate of sliced pieces of homemade pound cake on a plain yellow plate.

"So, my young Wimtje has returned," she said, as she took a seat across from me. "It's been so many years. How many years?"

"More than fifteen," I said.

She asked me about my life in Amsterdam. We carried on this casual chatter for some time. To that point, I had felt an awkward stranger in this town, which made it all the more pleasant to be with someone familiar. Her mind proved as sharp as ever, betraying no sign she was well past eighty. We reminisced about boyhood incidents I'd long forgotten. We talked about my father too and it touched me how much his memory still meant to her. The way she spoke made me wonder if more had occurred between them than I knew about.

"But tell me," she said, abruptly, "what on earth would bring you back to sleepy, humble, Leeuwarden? Certainly not to visit your old housekeeper and recount memories."

"I'm looking for the Zelle family," I said.

Mrs. Huizenga's eyebrows lifted briefly, inquiringly, but then drooped sadly.

"Sorry, I know all this time's passed, but it still breaks my heart. Poor, dear Antje . . ."

My hand jerked at hearing my daughter's name. If my teacup hadn't been on the table, I would have spilled it.

"I'm sorry, Mrs. Huizenga, who is Antje?"

She looked up, her eyes sad. "Why, Adam's wife, the mother, of course."

"Oh," I said, relieved yet eerily disturbed by the coincidence. Antje had been my instinctual choice for my daughter's name.

"Yes, of course, this all happened after you left. Anyway, with the separation, the money troubles, it all became too much for her and she became sick and . . ."

"Mrs. Zelle died?"

"You ought to have seen how distraught Antje's daughter was at her death, which struck me as quite remarkable and sweet, after her being so attached to her father all those years."

"You mean, Margaretha," I said, leaning forward.

"Of course, they only had the one girl—ah, now I understand. She's the object of your interest?"

I nodded. Mrs. Huizenga paused to eat a piece of cake, before continuing.

"Well that's no surprise, I suppose. All you boys were much too fond of her, encouraging her so, giving her all the attention she craved. She was a girl made for the stage, to be sure. If only she'd reined in the innocent flirtations of youth. Such a spoiled child too. I believe it was as much how Adam spoiled her as her own nature that made things turn out as they did."

"What do you mean turn out as they did?"

Mrs. Huizenga held up a hand and shook her head slightly, as if reluctant to tell me. Could she possibly know about Paris? But she'd only paused to swallow a piece of cake and wash it down with some tea.

"After her mother died, in 1891, M'Greet went to live, not with her father as she wished, but with an uncle and aunt in Sneek. I suspect she proved too much to handle for them. They sent her to a school that specialized in training kindergarten teachers."

"Kindergarten teacher?" I said.

"Yes, can you imagine her having to give all that attention, instead of receiving it?"

"No," I said, and we shared a brief chuckle before her face turned serious.

"There was some unpleasant business at that school, unfortunately. Depending on whom you talk to, the headmaster, a married man over fifty, fell in love with our Margaretha, or she with him. Too many contradictory versions to know what really happened. Nonetheless, a scandal ensued and the resulting shame to Margaretha was distressing."

I winced. My mind contemplated several scenarios, some of which indeed might have been worse than Paris.

"But what brings about this sudden interest in M'Greet?"

I hesitated. I had come to Leeuwarden ready to relate candidly to her family what I had discovered in Paris, and even to offer my help to extricate Maggie from that situation. But Mrs. Huizenga's obliviousness to the possibility and her regard for the Zelle family, put that idea out of my mind. In fact, it kept alive the slim hope I was wrong.

"Actually, I'm here because my Uncle Dick passed away recently."

"Oh yes, Dick Terpstra. I had read about that. I'm surprised you've remained in touch, I mean, after all that happened between them and your grandfather."

"Yes," I said, not really sure what she was talking about, "it seemed improper not to come and pay my respects."

"You were a difficult child but I always saw your father's sensibilities in you," she said, nodding approvingly. "And once you arrived here, nostalgia brought you back to your old neighbourhood?"

"No, it's not that. I was abroad recently, in Paris to be specific, and saw someone who reminded me of M'Greet. The resemblance was so startling I thought it might be her."

"Paris. My word."

"So you don't know where she is, or what she's doing?"

"I'm afraid not. I mean, I'd heard something about Den Haag, and possibly a marriage, but no, I've lost touch. Even if she were in Paris, I doubt I'd have heard about it. But why not ask her father? I'm sure he's still in Amsterdam."

"Her father?" I said. "Of course."

"Poor man," she said, standing up to rummage through some drawers. "People treated Adam Zelle harsher than he deserved. Ah, here you are. See him if you wish to find out more. And please say hello from me."

I nodded while taking the card bearing an Amsterdam address not far from my house.

"And if you happen to see Margaretha again, promise me you'll give her my love."

The way she said it, without irony and with sincere affection, affected me. Would she have said it in that way had she known what I knew, or suspected, about Maggie in Paris? There was no doubt in my mind she would have; Mrs. Huizenga always thought the best of people.

Outside, the leafless branches of several trees behind me dispersed the sun's brightness, creating odd shapes on the water. On one of the boathouses, a young woman was sweeping a deck while a caged parrot encouraged her with unintelligible squawks. Then the bird turned its head toward me, its cries sounding a warning for me to get away. It shook me until a plump orange cat came by and stopped to rub its head against my leg.

"Would you be the dissolute Lothario responsible for those orphaned kittens?" I said.

The cat began purring as I stroked the warm fur on its back. Perhaps displeased I had no food, the feline plodded away, toward the edge of the canal where it collapsed on a sunny spot on the concrete, next to a tree.

Aunt Josephine

I crossed through the center of town along a zigzag of narrow streets on my way toward the eastern canal. There I crossed a bridge onto the main road, the Vliet, where I came upon a row of plain, brown houses. I wandered around the area a few times, trying to stir up memories. Nothing. Then I heard a female voice behind me, clear, confident, youthful, and with the practical brevity that marked Frisian accents.

"Are you lost, sir?"

I turned around. A young woman stood alone, arms crossed, wearing a simple black dress down to her feet, covering the top of her wooden shoes. A pale yellow apron over the dress lessened the dour impression, but not much. Hatless, her thin blonde hair bundled in a mass, accenting the whiteness of her skin. And her eyes, a soft, captivating sea-blue surprised me with a vital spirit similar to my daughter's.

"Which would be the Terpstra residence?"

"Are you looking for anyone in particular?" she said, a challenging lilt in her voice.

"May I ask who you are?" I said.

"Once you offer the same information about yourself," she said, her expression bold, keen.

"My name is Wim Brink," I said, tipping my hat to hide my amusement.

"Oh my," she said, letting out a slight gasp, followed by a bemused smile.

"Now please be so kind as to—"

Before I could finish, this young lady took my arm, guided me inside a house, motioned for me to stay in a hallway I knew I had been in before. Confirming that, a dense but pleasant aroma from the kitchen, the wonderfully unmistakable mashing of potatoes, carrots, and onions into *hutspot*. No doubt made the way my father would make it, lavishly sprinkled with bacon bits and a horseshoe-shaped *rookworst*— smoked sausage—nestled in the middle and steaming. Ah, I hadn't enjoyed a simple, hearty Dutch meal for such a long time. Cornelia hated most Dutch dishes, particularly *hutspot*, so we rarely ate them at home.

"Ingrid, is that you?" an older woman's voice called out, stopping the girl halfway up the stairs.

"Mother, we have a guest."

"We do? Who is it?"

Ingrid looked down at me, a cue to answer. "It's Wim Brink," I said, reproaching myself for forgetting to bring flowers.

A faint, high-pitched sigh preceded heavy footsteps shuffling slowly down the stairs. My Aunt Josephine's hair had turned white. The sturdy woman from my fleeting memories now struggled to move about.

"You've grown so tall, nephew, but you have the same slender shoulders as your father. Here, let me take your coat—oh, I can tell by your fine clothes that you have prospered."

Aside from the disparaging way she had said, "prospered," I couldn't have hoped for a warmer welcome. My aunt directed me into the sitting room.

While it lacked the grandness of our rooms on the Herengracht in Amsterdam, this was a cozy space. Yet surprisingly large. There was an American style rocking chair and ottoman, made of light pine, and a sofa with two matching chairs, recently upholstered in a brown and green pattern. Tucked away in a corner, a small piano accentuated the room's intimacy. Thick red curtains and oriental rugs covered the hardwood flooring. Flowers in small pots filled the room, on end tables, on bookshelves, on the windowsill. A few hung from the ceiling.

Another odour superimposed the kitchen smells. An ancient, nostalgic mustiness from decades of sweet cigar smoke embedded in the rugs and walls. A vague reminiscence came to me of my Uncle Dick, with his cropped hair sitting back in the rocker puffing away at his pipe, while I played with wooden blocks or other toys on the rug. No ashtrays now though.

The bookshelves contained several volumes of encyclopaedias and reference books, and a large quantity of novels. Amongst respectable authors such as Jane Austen and Henry James, I noticed several by D. H. Lawrence and others whose works I'd consider inappropriate in a household of women. Most of the novels looked second-hand, many in the original English. On a lower shelf, I spotted a brand new but well used Dutch-English dictionary. I supposed they kept their Bible in a separate, special place. Several framed photographs of family members filled the gaps.

"This is a most unexpected surprise," my aunt said, motioning for me to sit on the sofa. Ingrid brought in a tea tray and began pouring for the three of us, my aunt watching over her. Then she took the seat next to me while Ingrid settled in one of the armchairs.

"I'm so sorry about Uncle Dick," I said.

I caught a tear rolling down Ingrid's cheek before she could turn to brush it away. Contrary to my initial impression, I now saw my cousin as quite pretty. How refreshing to encounter an attractive young lady wearing such modest attire without a trace of self-consciousness.

"So you received our sad announcement," Ingrid said.

"Unfortunately only yesterday, I'm afraid. I was away on business."

"I see," my aunt said. "We understand, of course. You missed a lovely ceremony, small but tasteful, just the way Dick would have wanted. And he has a lovely plot in Spanjaardslaan. But please don't feel bad. When it comes to family, it's never too late."

I smiled to show my appreciation for her understanding. "How did he die?" I said.

"It was his time to go," my aunt said. "Our grief will run its course eventually and blossom into a wonderful memory for he was a wonderful man." She paused. "Speaking of blossoming, let us talk about you, looking like a nobleman, so refined."

She said the word, "refined," as she had said, "prospered," earlier, with an odd, almost sarcastic inflection. As if I was a mass-produced item, overly polished, ostentatious even, made to look hand crafted. I glanced down at my black suit. Expertly tailored, yes, but rather unexceptional compared to others I owned; and the blue tie and gold clip I had brought with me were not my finest.

"You've come by yourself?" Ingrid said.

"Well, yes, but my wife, Cornelia, sends her condolences."

"Well, that's always nice to hear, even if from someone we've never met," my aunt said.

Good manners compelled me not to risk misinterpreting this. But the longer the ensuing silence, the harder that became. Only then did I begin to recall my grandfather's admonitions to forget everything about my life in Leeuwarden. No wonder my return had sparked no memories within me. I took Opa Geert's comments in stride long ago, never questioning them, never considering how the objects of his disdain— which now seemed so blatant—might feel.

"Please don't mind my mother. Certain memories—"

"I heard your father's father passed on several years ago?" Aunt Josephine said.

"Yes, he and Oma Isabel died within weeks of each other. Like Uncle Dick. Of old age."

"It's obvious they took good care of you in the meantime," my aunt said, matter-of-factly.

"Thank you, I like to think they did."

My aunt's eyes betrayed her scepticism and her look unsettled me. I was tempted to boast of the fine private schools I had attended, how my studiousness had qualified me for the esteemed Leiden University, and then how Opa Geert's friendship and business dealings with the van Rozebouts had led to my marriage to Cornelia, which had earned me my high position in the company, my fine office at the Beurs. Instead, I reached into my shirt pocket to retrieve the tiny studio portrait of my daughter taken this past Christmas. It showed Antje, wearing a specially tailored white dress that accentuated her blonde curls, clutching her favourite porcelain doll. I passed the photograph to Ingrid first. She studied it for some time before handing it to her mother.

"How adorable," my aunt said, her face flushing from a warm smile.

"She's a miracle," I said, not only because I truly felt so, but also because Antje's picture seemed to have eased the present tension.

"I imagine you are a fine father too, Wim. I hope you let her meet her poor relatives in the north someday. Your wife too, of course . . . Ingrid dear, do you mind . . ."

Without another word, my cousin cleared the table, returning with three cups of steaming hot pea soup, and a plate of crackers and rolls. I noticed how my aunt regarded her daughter with pride. That deep bond between mother and child appeared so natural and effortless. I wondered how Uncle Dick and Ingrid had related as father and daughter. Her grief, still fresh judging by the tear I had witnessed earlier, indicated a closeness I hoped I would always share with my daughter.

Ingrid's return brought about an awkward silence of a different type, as when people who ought to be acquainted realize they are, in fact, strangers. Thank goodness for the soup, which happened to be delicious.

"So, Wim, if your Uncle Dick hadn't passed away, you would never have come here, would you?" my aunt said, her voice stern, her eyes shrewd.

"Oh, Mother, stop berating him. He's here, isn't he?"

My aunt shrugged as she finished her soup, and then motioned for Ingrid to refill it. She pointed at mine but I refused.

"Perhaps I'd better get going," I said.

My aunt made no objection, gave no indication she wished for me to stay for supper, which smelled even better now. I hated to leave with matters unsettled but felt I had done what I could. Ingrid accompanied me outside, shutting the door behind her.

"I'm sorry about all that," my cousin said.

"I came to pay my respects for Uncle Dick."

"Of course, we know that. It may not appear so, but my mother is extremely pleased you came. Shocked too. Put yourself in her position. What if you unexpectedly encountered someone face to face whom you hadn't seen for so long?"

Her question stabbed me with its accidental perceptiveness. "I see your point," I said.

"Good. Now please join us for dinner tomorrow."

"I'm afraid I will be return to Amsterdam this evening."

"Don't leave just yet. Now that you've come to us, I don't want you to leave with anything but the best feelings. Give me a chance, give us a chance, let us make a better impression on you before you go home."

So charming. Ingrid was precisely the type of young woman I'd want Antje to take after. I envisioned my cousin as an active role model for my daughter. But if I didn't stay, there was a chance we'd never see each other again.

"All right," I said.

"Wonderful."

"By the way, Ingrid, do you know anyone by the name of Zelle? The father operated a hat shop on the Kelders."

"Oh," she said, and her demeanour fell. It took me a moment to grasp the insensitivity of my query, how it implied my visit to the Terpstras was of secondary interest. But she regained her composure before I could explain. "No, I don't know them. Who are they?"

"Just old acquaintances," I said, trying to remain casual, although inwardly relieved. "People I thought I might look up while I was in Leeuwarden."

"I've never heard of them. We could ask Mother."

"No, that's all right," I said, for my aunt would most certainly see through my deception.

"As you wish, my long lost cousin. Now may I ask you a question?"

"Of course."

Her eyes rolled up to look at the clouds.

"Do you miss New York?"

It took a moment to realize she had spoken in English, the syllables affected by that harsh Frisian accent. Then I recalled the Dutch-English dictionary and the English novels on the bookshelves. Behind her modesty, there was something pressing; this was no idle inquiry.

The quick answer was no, not anymore, but the mention of the city of my birth, combined with the enthusiasm in her voice, sparked a collage of varied memories. Tall buildings, the grids of straight streets and avenues, the people, the harbour. Excursions with my father to Staten Island and the Statue of Liberty, and getting lost in Central Park. Then there were the memories of friends, of going to school and getting into fights over the pettiest matters.

"That's more than eighteen years ago, a stage of my life that no longer has much meaning for me," I said. "I don't think of it enough to miss it, do you know what I mean?"

I wasn't sure if that was an accurate reflection of how I felt. Just because I never thought of New York enough to miss it didn't mean it had lost all meaning, did it?

"So you have no desire to go back?" she said, returning to Dutch. It was as much a mild accusation as question.

"Go back?" I said. "No, why would I?"

"I'm sorry. I didn't know this would be a sensitive subject for you. Please forgive me."

"No, it's not that," I said, but could think of nothing further to add.

"But you are going to come back and see us tomorrow," she said.

"Do you doubt my word?" I said, as a joke, but she took a step back.

"Of course not. Sorry. I'm afraid I didn't express myself properly. I don't want you to see it as an obligation or an appointment. I want it to be that you truly want to come back to see us. Because that's how we feel, how I feel."

Her plea helped because my aunt's less-than-warm welcome still wasn't sitting well with me.

"I'm going straight to my hotel," I said, gravely, "to reserve another night and telegram my wife that I will stay another day."

"Thank you."

The following morning I found myself in rubber boots, standing atop a mushy knoll of parsley-coloured grass, gazing out over the grey-blue expanse of the North Sea. Behind me and around me simple wooden fences corralled dozens of grey and cream-coloured sheep. Impervious to the cold, they grazed along the damp, dark green plains between several *terpen*, those unique villages built on mounds of mud to withstand floods. The faint smell of pasture triggered even fainter memories. I had been here before, with someone. Perhaps Uncle Dick. It had to have been Uncle Dick, as my father had such a morbid fear of water.

A brisk wind pounded chilly salt air against me, inciting shivers despite the Shetland wool sweater and warm boots I had borrowed from the hotel clerk. After reserving an extra night at the hotel, and sending two telegrams—one to Cornelia and the other to my office—I had asked the clerk what one could do for recreation hereabouts. He had recommended a small excursion one of the guests had arranged to see the dykes. The omnibus would leave promptly at six o'clock in the morning, returning to Leeuwarden by early afternoon. Plenty of time to prepare for my dinner with the Terpstras.

Through the mist-obscured horizon across the harsh sea, I could faintly make out the long, skinny outlines of two of the Frisian Islands, Ameland and Terschelling. A combination of engine trouble and inclement weather had cancelled the ferry crossing to Ameland that was part of the tour. I didn't mind for I was content to take in the countryside and its raw beauty.

"Wonderful, isn't it, Mr. Brink, this fresh sea air," a man said to me, in English. It took a moment to identify the speaker as Mark Dekker, a director of a rival shipping company whom I had met in Marseille. Not the most handsome fellow, because of that sallow face and slightly hooked nose. Not tall either. But he carried himself with confidence and dignity. He must have been in the rear of the omnibus behind the large German couple for me not to have noticed him earlier. "Not quite the exotic agreeability of the Mediterranean," he added, "but heartier, wouldn't you say?"

"No hard feelings, I hope," I said, as we shook hands. "About Marseille."

I was referring to how several aggressive van Rozebout bids had won over the business from some of Mark's customers, redirecting their shipping services through Rotterdam and Amsterdam instead of southern France.

"Business is business," he said, with no trace of resentment, although my father-in-law and the owner of his firm had exchanged heated words once or twice. "We were losing our hold on those clients—you'll find them awfully demanding, by the way—and we had expected to lose them. Although, I must say, I didn't expect it would be to old van Rozebout."

"Oh?"

"Whatever's happened to the son, Max?"

"My brother-in-law?" I said.

"Ah, I see," Mark said. "Glad to know the van Rozebout penchant for nepotism is alive and well. At least the old man got it right this time in taking you. I doubt Max could have pulled those negotiations off the way you did. Charming fellow but his business sense . . ."

"Thank you," I said, humbly, but inwardly pleased. "Max helps out occasionally but he is no longer with the company officially."

"Oh? What does he do then?"

"He lives in Paris."

Mark paused as if expecting me to say more but there was nothing more to say.

"Are you setting sights on our North Sea interests now?" Mark then said, with a smile. "Should I warn my colleagues they might see you in Hamburg next week?"

"No, not at all," I said, smiling. "I'm here visiting relatives." It sounded convincing, and it was even true, yet it still felt like a lie and saying it made me uncomfortable. "The sea air really clears the mind," I said, hoping I could change the subject.

"But it does make one cold, and hungry."

I agreed. Mark and I then trod along a path of alternately hard and soft ground. It took nearly twenty minutes to cover the half-mile to the village restaurant. Its wonderful hearth and friendly service made it worth the effort. With that crisp air coursing through me, I opted for the herring, freshly salted and recently caught from the North Sea. Mark joined me in sliding several skinny fish simultaneously, much to the amusement of the other patrons—the young Bavarian couple from our tour and two local fellows who must have been brothers, if not twins—who had come into the restaurant behind us.

We drank coffee and enjoyed an intimate chat. An American now, but born and raised in Groningen, Mark left Holland when only nine. In many ways, his past mirrored mine. After our encounters in Marseille, he had travelled all the way up the Rhine into Holland, stopping briefly in Friesland to visit relatives before wrapping up his trip in Germany. The highlight of our talk was his fascinating description of Roosevelt's inauguration, which he had the good fortune of attending just before coming to Europe.

"An impressive man," he concluded. "A beacon for America's future, I reckon."

"I don't doubt it," I said.

"So you have no interest in ever returning to the United States?" he said.

"Funny," I said, with a chuckle, "you're the second person in the past twenty-four hours to ask me that." I then explained Ingrid's curiosity about America.

"If your cousin wishes to know anything then by all means have her write," he said, handing me a contact card. "And we're always looking for top people in Boston too, should you ever wish to explore other opportunities. For yourself, I mean, not your company."

"When are you going back?" I said, pocketing the card, and handing him mine.

"In a few weeks, middle of April, I expect."

"Your wife and family must miss you."

He hesitated, before shaking his head. "Perhaps some day."

For a brief moment I was tempted to invite the bachelor to the Terpstras for dinner. But it would have been too presumptuous in too many ways. Cornelia could have pulled it off, not me.

"We ought to return to the bus," I said, checking my watch. Mark nodded, and we both put on our coats.

The walk back took longer than it should have. The driver glared at us for being late, and then again for muddying the inside of his vehicle with our boots.

The return was slow going but eventually the spires of Grote Kerk and Saint Boniface came into view, albeit from an unexpected angle. Apparently, we had taken an alternate route back. Soon we came upon a rather large park. I asked the driver what it was.

"That's Spanjaardslaan cemetery."

"You don't say. Can you stop here?"

"Sir, we cannot stop, I must return no later than two o'clock. I'm already behind schedule."

"Just let me out then. You don't have to wait for me."

"What's here?" Mark asked.

"A grave I want to visit."

The driver gave me a strange look as he reluctantly stopped the vehicle. It looked like Mark might want to accompany me but instead he offered to have a cab come pick me up when he got back to the hotel. I gratefully accepted. His kindness put the idea of inviting him to the Terpstras for dinner back in my mind, but the driver's impatience thwarted that. The bus was on its way the moment my feet hit the ground.

A worker pointed me to Uncle Dick's grave. The ground around it was damp but not as trampled as in other parts of the cemetery. It stood alone, separated from batches of family plots. There was an empty spot, presumably set aside for my aunt. Then it struck me how odd it seemed that my father's grave wasn't here, but in Amsterdam.

Recent mud had collected in the inscribed letters and numbers of the temporary headstone. I dirtied my hands to brush it off. Doing so felt good. As did finding a woman with a cart selling flowers. I purchased a colourful nosegay and placed it against the stone before kneeling to pray. I thanked the Lord for reuniting me with Aunt Josephine and Ingrid, and then asked for blessings for their future and that of everyone I knew, including Maggie, but especially my innocent daughter.

Ingrid answered the door wearing a blue dress of a silk-like material with streaky vertical tinges of pink. Unlike what she wore the other day, this dress was not homemade. Still, I could not help viewing her attire from Cornelia's perspective, as shabby. Then again, I could never picture my cousin wearing any of my wife's immodest clothes. I handed over a bouquet of flowers and two bottles of wine I had purchased on the way. I thought again of Mark Dekker; it seemed a shame such a charming girl was not already married or engaged.

A delicious odour of herring and eel, and a sharper scent that was probably some kind of mustard, interrupted this thought. My aunt came out to greet me, wiping her hands on a large white apron covering a finely pleated green dress. While she didn't expressly offer an apology, I sensed contrition in her manner. After our greeting, she left, but returned a moment later with her apron gone and a bottle of *Jenever* and two glasses in her hands.

"Your Uncle Dick always enjoyed a *borrel* before dinner," my aunt said.

"As did Opa Geert," I said, without thinking.

This brought no reaction other than a slight harrumph as my aunt set the glasses and bottle on the coffee table and poured. She glanced at me before taking a sip. I did the same but then struggled to stifle a reaction; the brand lacked the quality I was accustomed to. Its effect, on the other hand, was quite powerful.

"Are you not having any?" I said, to Ingrid.

"I only drink wine, and, should the occasion ever arise, I would love to try champagne."

"Oh, Ingrid," my aunt said. It wasn't clear to me if she was disappointed or amused.

"Aunt Josephine," I said, my nerve bolstered by the alcohol, "will you tell me why you despise my grandfather?"

"Let's talk of pleasant matters first," my aunt said, "while Ingrid and I finish preparing dinner."

Then she rose and left me with the bottle. My aunt and cousin undertook the preparations in setting the table and checking the cooking, alternately pausing on their trips between the kitchen and dining area to chat. When I told them about my excursion to the dykes—I left out the part about having eaten herring already—Ingrid's face brightened.

"I wish you'd asked me to join you."

"Ingrid!" my aunt said.

"Actually, I wasn't alone, and it might have been a good idea if you had come," I said.

"Oh?" Ingrid said.

"Yes. I met this fine fellow—"

"No, mother was right. I shouldn't have been so forward. I apologize."

"And don't interrupt either. Sorry, Wim, you were saying you met someone."

"That's all right, I was rambling," I said.

"Your Uncle Dick loved to go up to the top of the country, as he would always say. He took the two of you children along once, even, but Ingrid you cried so much you had to wait in the carriage."

"Mother, please."

"Dick would have taken you up there as often as you'd have liked, if given the chance."

"I think I remembered that time when I was up there today," I said.

"That's sweet," my aunt said.

"Yes, and on the way back, I stopped at Spanjaardslaan. I put some flowers on Uncle Dick's grave."

My aunt said nothing but I could see she was pleased.

"So, did you find those Zelle people you were looking for?" Ingrid said. "I asked some friends but no one knew them."

"I—No, I think they've all left Leeuwarden," I said, feeling my face redden, regretting mentioning it at all the day before.

"Who is this?" my aunt said.

"Mother, do you know any Zelle?"

"The haberdasher?" she said.

"Yes," Ingrid and I said, together.

"Your father knew him, Ingrid, although I never met the man, or his family. Once Dick told me he was a freemason, I lost all interest."

"A freemason?" Ingrid and I said, again in unison, which made my aunt laugh.

"Actually, it turned out he wasn't. He tried but they wouldn't accept him."

"Why not?" I said.

"I have no idea, dear nephew. I don't even know why I remember that detail. But why would such a man be of interest to you?"

"A business matter, something probably best not to discuss while we eat," I said.

This drew a wry glance from both of them before they left to finish preparations. During the meal, talk was limited, our mouths occupied with the fine food. The herring wasn't as fresh as what I had had earlier, but the way it was prepared made it taste better.

After, while my aunt and cousin cleared the table, I sat alone in the main room, anxiously awaiting their return. But the longer they took, the more my curiosity and need for answers diminished. What was the point of stirring up history when there was so much possibility for the future? How heartening it was going to be for Antje to have more relatives to dote on her, to show her one could be happy without wealth. Whatever animosity my aunt felt for Opa Geert and whatever Opa Geert had done to cause such feelings shouldn't affect our current lives, I reasoned.

But when Aunt Josephine returned, she seemed intent on settling matters now. Ingrid came in right after with a tea tray and poured us each a cup. My aunt hesitated slightly, perhaps to check her tone.

"Tell me, Wim, haven't you ever wondered about us?" I looked over at Ingrid but this time my cousin was not coming to my defence. Now it seemed the death announcement had been an invitation to an ambush. As if sensing my discomfort, my aunt put a hand on my knee. "Please, please be honest."

"I did wonder, occasionally, but after so many years out of touch, well, I suppose not. And my grandfather never encouraged looking back to the past."

My aunt sat back and nodded, satisfied with my response. "What do you remember about the period after your father's death?"

"Very little," I said, quickly but truthfully.

"Will you listen to what I have to say then, how I want to say it, and defer your reaction?"

I nodded.

After my father's death, she began, my aunt and Uncle Dick took steps to become my legal guardians, with the intention of adopting me later on. The paperwork was signed and awaiting official stamping when my grandfather showed up in Leeuwarden with two lawyers.

"We'd barely heard of the man before. We knew about the nasty falling out in the 1860s when Hans—I mean your father—went to America to fight in that slavery war. And that the rift worsened when your father came back and chose to move up to Leeuwarden instead of Amsterdam. Therefore Geert wasn't around for your father marrying Dick's sister—I'm sure he'd have disapproved of Beatrix anyway—and I doubted he knew your father and mother had gone to America—that was 1875—or even that your mother died two years later, until Hans returned with you in '87. Geert did make an attempt then to mend matters. Only your father preferred to keep your grandfather out of your life. And would have to this day were he still alive. I sincerely believed that then and I still do today."

My aunt paused, either to compose herself or to give me a moment to absorb this. Her words rang true as I also never knew of my grandfather until after my father died. She took a sip of her tea but it must have been cold for she put it back down, scowling.

"The nerve of that man, showing up that way, with all his money and pride. Do you know he confronted us, right here in our own home, while you were upstairs sleeping? He and Dick got into a vicious row during which Geert implied we were kidnappers."

My aunt became too upset to go on and Ingrid took over.

"Wim, your Opa Geert argued, convincingly, that his direct blood lineage, as much as his wealth put him in the best position to raise you."

"His wealth," my aunt said with disdain. "Yet he didn't contribute a single guilder toward Hans's funeral, even though he insisted your father be buried in Amsterdam. That's where all what remained of your father's money went."

"Honestly, I don't remember any of that."

"I can see that, now," my aunt said, drying her eyes with a cloth. "What was worse was that Geert stayed until the police came and he virtually ordered them to take you away from us, only to put you with a strange family in Harlingen for a few days until the matter was settled."

"How sad," Ingrid said.

"Honestly, I don't remember anything about living in Harlingen."

"I meant that becoming an orphan is sad," Ingrid said.

"You see," my aunt said, "Ingrid works with orphans every day at a special school."

"How nice," I said, sincerely, but then added, "But honestly, from personal experience, it's not an unrecoverable setback in life."

They said nothing to this. Now I felt it my duty to respond to my aunt's vilification of a man who'd raised an insignificant, sinful and sometimes violent boy from a humble, turbulent youth and turned him into a solid, poised Christian gentleman.

"Opa Geert was very good to me," I said, trying not to sound too confrontational. "He put me in a challenging private school, but one in which there were plenty of activities—sports, chess, Bible studies—that I had no time to reflect on things in the past. And if not for him, I'd never have met my wife—"

"An enriched life," my aunt said, with a tinge of sarcasm.

"—or had my daughter," I added.

"You know Wim, it was never a question of whether your grandfather could provide for you. In that regard, we conceded his superiority. Living with him made sense, and we would not have objected had he not called us poor, backward farmers, and heaped such scorn on us. Such hatred and prejudice seemed to us a poor influence for a young man, regardless of material advantages. And what was the point of severing all ties with us? Believe me, we tried to contact you, often. To my dying day I'll swear your father would have never allowed any of that to happen."

"I turned out fine," I said, unable to still the trembling in my voice.

"I think you would have turned out fine with us too."

"I didn't mean it that way. And I'm not sure you're right about my father. I was too much for him. You should have seen me in New York. I was a terrible child, always getting into trouble, and I'm sure I was the reason my father and I moved back to Holland. For all I know, he intended to hand me over to Opa Geert even before he died, even if it meant separation. I needed the discipline that much."

"Yes, you did, especially after how you beat up that poor Bart Postma over some girl. We knew that boy's parents well—wait, what was that girl's name? Could it have been . . .?"

"Aunt Josephine, you were saying."

"Anyway, you raise a good point. It's clear to me wealth has not spoiled you. Quite the contrary. You've benefited from a fine university education. You've married a noble lady. I'm glad to see we were proven wrong."

"Do you mean that?" I said.

"Yes I do. For me, the saddest part is we didn't even get a chance to try, or even to say goodbye. Geert vowed to keep you away from the Terpstra influence. And he did."

"Until now," I said.

"Yes, until now," my aunt said, wiping away some tears.

Tears always distressed me but these were happy ones, a reward even. This heart-warming reunion with two fine ladies put the distressing thoughts of Maggie and Mata Hari far back in my mind. I put my arm around my aunt who then embraced me. But when we separated, she sniffed once to collect herself, perhaps afraid of showing too much sentimentality in front of her daughter. Ingrid seemed unmoved by it all and was watching us, much in the way Antje watched Cornelia and I during our rows.

"Ingrid, honey, play something for us."

Needing no encouragement, my cousin opened up the piano, tapped a few keys as a test, and then played a series of delightful songs, popular, current tunes, simple ones with bright melodies. She played them quite well and the music dissipated the lingering tension in the room. While Ingrid played, my aunt and I talked of small things, such as the differences in lifestyles between Amsterdam and Leeuwarden and other cities.

"I find cities fascinating," Ingrid said, not missing a note.

"As with anything, they have their good points and bad points," I said.

"I'd love to travel and see more, London, Paris . . . and especially America."

"All right, Ingrid, all right. That's enough. You are too impossible at times."

Ingrid stopped playing, the echo of a sombre note trailing off into silence.

"You seem particularly infatuated with the United States, Ingrid," I said.

"My daughter has this notion of emigrating to America, someday."

"It's more than a notion, Mother."

"Not to me it isn't, not yet."

My cousin dropped her head, said nothing.

"But when?" I said. "Why?"

"Why? Ingrid expects to find a better life there than in Europe. I have reluctantly agreed not to oppose her, because she may be right. You see, we've had poor luck with suitors. As far as when, well . . ."

"I'm going as soon as I can. I hope to depart before the end of the summer, perhaps in

August. Sooner if possible, maybe even after my birthday at the end of May."

"She is still, in my opinion, too young. And I don't think we've tried hard enough to settle you here yet."

"We have most certainly tried hard enough. What would you have me do next? Insert an advertisement in the Courant? There is no one, in Leeuwarden, in Europe, or in the world, for all I know."

My aunt flashed me a look of exasperation, or was it an appeal? Did she hope to pass responsibility for Ingrid's future to me, as the sole male kin in the Terpstra family? While I found my cousin's determination appealing, the threat of separation in only a few months dejected me. Those images of Ingrid playing with Antje, teaching my daughter useful things, were now vanishing.

"I need to save money and keep improving my English," she said.

"Ingrid! How dare you?"

"What, mother?"

My aunt turned to me. "I must apologize for my daughter, if that came out as an appeal for financial help."

"I didn't mean it that way," Ingrid said.

"I didn't take it that way," I said.

"Nephew, promise me you will not donate a single *stuiver*, toward this enterprise."

"Mother, I don't want anyone's money. I'll earn it myself. I'm close to having enough for a third-class ticket. Now I just need enough to live on for a month or two."

"What do you intend to do in the America?"

Ingrid paused to measure her response.

"I'm not sure yet. Just as I'm not sure what I would do here either. America strikes me as a better place to be unsure than Europe."

"Your father would forbid it."

"You may be right about that, mother, but you may be wrong too."

"I am not wrong about that."

"And you intend to undertake this alone?" I said.

"Alone, yes, just like thousands of other emigrants."

"In steerage?"

"You see, even your cousin, who's only known you two days, sees the folly in this," my aunt said.

"Nonsense mother, he didn't mean it that way. He was just asking, weren't you?"

"Ingrid, don't pressure our guest like that."

My aunt turned to me, her eyes seeming to appeal to me to contradict her daughter.

"As a parent myself, I can't say I'd be comfortable about my pretty daughter making such a voyage unaccompanied."

"That's right," my aunt said.

"Well then, perhaps you can accompany me, my cousin, or find someone who can," Ingrid said, a twinkle in her eye.

"Ingrid! This is too much."

My cousin's audacity, clearly in jest, amused me, although I suppressed my smile when my aunt glared at her daughter.

Cornelia

It was nearing the end of the workday. A lovely afternoon, the sky unimpeded by clouds. The sun's light flickered intermittently in a most fascinating way, dancing patterns as it shone through my office window blinds. As a candle might in nervous hands, casting erratic yellowy spots on my antique Captain's desk and its contents. Unlike the sky, the fine but scuffed teak was barely visible under piles of memos, invoices, contracts, and other documents requiring my perusal or signature. The clamour of merchants' calls, horses' hooves, vendors' carts, and a street organ on the Damrak below created a melodic commotion of energetic purposefulness.

The previous month's excursion to Marseille had proved a tremendous success for the van Rozebout Shipping Company, far beyond my preliminary estimations. Naturally, that meant a corresponding increase in my responsibilities, which had become almost overwhelming. Not in complexity, but in quantity. Hiring new staff, training them, assigning them, refining our processes, recasting budgets, and so forth: it was energizing and enervating at the same time. One benefit, I was too distracted to think of Maggie or Mata Hari; the downside being the same applied to my aunt and cousin in Leeuwarden.

With all that work to be done, it seemed too quiet in the outer office. I opened my door to discover rows of unoccupied desks and chairs, my staff huddled around Jaap Vos's desk. He was the most experienced on my staff, and one of the least disciplined. No doubt he and his colleagues were debating the location of their after work drink, without a single notion of inviting their employer.

The young men who worked for me, all in their mid-twenties to mid-thirties, with mixed ambitions and potential, were friendly enough with their superior but never in the easy way as with each other. Even the most recent hires acted more at ease than I felt I could. No doubt my filial connection to the van Rozebout family had something to do with it. From a personal standpoint this sometimes bothered me, but from a professional one it was preferable. Detachment between employer and employee was essential to productivity; it made it easier to apply strictness, when necessary. I stepped away from my desk to do just that.

"Even more beautiful in person, so I'm told," Jaap was saying. "We'll be sure to tell you boys all about it when we come back."

"I only hope we will be able to obtain tickets," Thijs said.

Thijs Vollmer was one of my recent hires, a fine-looking twenty-three-year-old from a respectable, if not wealthy, family. He had recently graduated with honours from Leiden University, my alma mater. Thijs had a promising future with our company. To see him engaging in idle chatter this way was disconcerting, to discover him consorting with Jaap more so.

"We won't know unless we try," Jaap said.

"Tickets to what?" I said, forced to raise my voice above the aggregated muttering coming from the other men.

Their faces betrayed the discomfort of guilty surprise. Two fellows stepped aside to give me a clearer view of Jaap's desk. Surrounded by a clutter of pens and clips and staples, covering most of the desk, an opened copy of the British paper, *News of the Day*.

While we advertised in one or two London dailies, and subscribed to others, I didn't think this was one. My eyes scrolled from the banner to a full-page feature on Mata Hari, highlighted by a photograph of questionable taste. In this one, she looked more like Maggie than she had at the Guimet.

I suppressed a reflex reaction as I skimmed the article's contents. The writer did little more than restate the material I'd read in Paris back in March. But at the end, he posed the question, "Who can Mata Hari be?" I was stunned and felt as if a spotlight was shining on me.

"Weren't you in France last month, sir?" Jaap said. "Apparently, her debut made quite a stir in Paris right about then?"

"That's right," Thijs said. "March 13, as the article states. I remember you left me in charge that day, Jaap, because you had to leave early to—"

Jaap shook his head, quieting Thijs, and everyone. Normally this would have piqued my attention and I'd have taken them aside to discern what had happened, and then most likely reproached them. But the article had taken me aback.

"It's true, isn't it, Mr Brink?" Jaap said, with renewed confidence when I kept quiet. "You were in France then, weren't you? You must have heard about her, or read about her. She was in all the papers."

For a brief instant, I was not their boss but a friend, a confidante. A sudden yearning for camaraderie almost overcame my good sense, tempting me to share what I knew and boast of my connection. Instead, I pointed at the last line.

"Who do you think she is?" I said, to no one in particular.

Their silence amused me. At any moment, I expected that invitation to join them for that beer after work. Until Jaap Vos moved the paper to reveal a much smaller clipping.

"Actually, Mr. Brink, that article is from yesterday's edition. I just had it out for the picture. An anonymous person sent in this response."

He handed me the clipping, a letter to the editor. According to its author, Mata Hari was really a Mrs. MacLeod, married to an English officer, but born and raised in Java. In her youth, she risked her life by infiltrating sacred Indian temples where she learned to dance without inhibition. Because of her natural talent, her unique posture and poses, the priests came to regard her as a holy dancer.

The little biography, or rather the fictional fantasy, sounded like an adult version of something the Maggie I used to know might have imagined. Indeed, I feared she had penned this particular item. I glanced at the photo again and then up at Thijs and, for some reason, an image of Bart Postma came to mind.

"Are you all right, sir?" Thijs said.

"I think, gentlemen, it is time we resumed our work," I said. "As you have all read in Mr. van Rozebout's latest memo, we are behind in our receivables. Without money coming in, money can't go out to pay for such things as wages. Please ponder these unsavoury matters on your own time of which, over the next few months, you'll have little. And whatever time you do have, I suggest you spend on more dignified pursuits."

I ignored the low grumbling that came when I crumpled up the response and discarded it and the article into the trash. Once the familiar hum of administration started up again, I returned to be alone in my office, where I brooded for some time on what I'd read and its implications. Mata Hari, instead of fading away as I had hoped, had become famous enough to warrant coverage in a British newspaper, not to mention inspiring men in Holland to take trips to Paris to see her. She was becoming, had become, a phenomenon.

Later, I called in Thijs and Jaap. They barely reacted when I told them that, due to the workload, they would have to cancel or postpone their trip to Paris. They accepted this rather stoically, and I knew this decision would permanently sever any hopes of bonding with my staff socially.

I then reached into my desk and rummaged through until I found the piece of paper Mrs. Huizenga had given me.

I stood in front of the dark brick house at Lange Leidsedwaarstraat 148. Although in decent condition, a far cry from the elegance of the Grote Kerkstraat home Adam Zelle had owned in Leeuwarden. Indeed, the building was not a house at all, but divided into apartments, much like the Zelle home on the Willemskade. I knocked at the door indicated for Zelle, A., fearing, or perhaps hoping, Maggie's father had moved.

An older man answered. He was of the same average height, and had the same thin, long, bearded face of the Mr. Zelle I vaguely remembered. At certain angles, his appearance reminded me of Abraham Lincoln, albeit without the powerfully solemn confidence. Plenty of arrogance and pomposity though. He puffed out his chest and stroked his beard as if trying to weed out the grey hairs.

"Yes, may I help you?"

"Good day, Mr. Zelle, I'm Wim Brink." I paused to see if he would recognize the name.

His face remained blank. "I was hoping to speak to you about Mag—M'Greet."

His eyes brightened briefly but then his expression became sceptical. "Has something happened to my daughter?"

The concern in his voice, so natural for any father, warned me he might not be receptive to what I had to say as me. My hesitation made him stiffen.

"You are a journalist? A lawyer? Or are you from the police? Did her husband send you?"

"The police?" I said. "No sir, none of that. In fact, I'm an old friend of your daughter's, from Leeuwarden. My father bought his hats from your shop on the Kelders."

This produced a melancholic smile, in which I noted a closer resemblance to his daughter than I ever had before. A woman's scolding voice called out something from behind him. He glanced up at the clear sky, pointed down the street.

"Let's share a beer somewhere and talk privately," he said.

We walked toward the Leidseplein, stopping at a tiny cafe with one empty table outside with one chair. Mr. Zelle bid me to take it while he went inside and found another chair and brought it out. With the sun shining brightly now, I felt hot in my black suit, and would have preferred to go inside.

A chubby man wearing an apron, carrying two bottles of beer and two glasses, approached our table. Mr. Zelle acted like an old and welcome patron although I got the impression the owner thought him a nuisance. The owner poured half a bottle into each glass and stood waiting, without comment. A slight nod from Maggie's father was my hint to hand over some money. I obliged and then the man left us alone.

"So you are M'Greet's friend," Zelle said, grandly, after taking a large sip. I nodded, somewhat guardedly, unsure how to interpret his tone. "You're not a friend of MacLeod's?" he said, suspicious again.

MacLeod. My heart sank hearing that name again. First Max, through Eric, then the article at the office. It sealed the last crack of doubt. No longer could I pretend the dancer was not my Maggie.

"Are you all right, young fellow? You look rather pale."

"Yes, I'm fine," I lied. "Who is MacLeod?"

"Her rotten, good-for-nothing husband," he said, with bitterness. "Sorry, I meant to say her rotten, good-for-nothing former husband."

"I see," I said. But now I was unsure how to lead the conversation. Former husband? Did that change anything? Zelle seemed relaxed now, comfortable. I wished I had never come, wished I could get up and leave.

"So how do you know my daughter?"

I told him about how I would talk to her after church, how I lived near his family.

"Ah yes, the Willemskade. No wonder I don't recall your name. Things were not good for me back then, but I suppose you must have heard plenty about that. Everyone talked of me, as if there were no better topics. Maybe there weren't—but you said you have news about M'Greet. You have seen her?"

I coughed away my embarrassment, recalling how Maggie used to induce such reactions in me too.

"Yes, I saw her, earlier this week, in Paris."

"Paris. Of course. Did you speak to her?"

"No, I mean, she was dancing on a stage . . ."

"Ah, that must have been some shock, eh? She performed beautifully, no?"

"You are aware of what she does in Paris?"

"My daughter and I have no secrets."

Quietly, I sipped my beer, flustered by the pride in his voice. Was it sincere or just fatherly delusion? I stared at him, he stared back at me. I tried to imagine our situations reversed, with a stranger bringing such news to me about Antje. The idea made me shudder.

Then I realized his stare had nothing to do with M'Greet, but something immediate. He nodded at his near empty glass. I emptied my pocket and put several few guilders in the center of the table. He took a few of the coins, his glass, and the two empty bottles inside the café. When he returned, with fresh beer, his face was serious.

"I sense you disapprove of what M'Greet is doing."

"I'm surprised you approve."

"Please don't interpret my reaction as approval. I would prefer she were married to a nobleman, or at least someone of importance, and raising a family. A fine looking fellow like you, that's what she deserves. Unfortunately, such a destiny may not be for her. I can accept that. No matter what she does, I will never forsake my daughter."

"I have a baby daughter too and—"

"And so you see what I mean."

"Yes."

A lie. I didn't see what he meant at all, never could, never would. I could never tolerate such degradation in my daughter. I wanted to badger him and discover how he had let this happen. I was looking for someone to blame; he was the natural candidate. We sat in silence for several minutes before I decided to take a different approach.

"You had the finest shop in Leeuwarden, everyone always said so, as I recall." He smiled at that. "My father always admired it and often pointed it out to me when we walked on the Kelders." I paused then and he nodded. I had broken his sullen mood, my appeal to his vanity working as it often did with Maggie. "Maybe you can tell me more about your daughter," I went on, "we lost touch just before she went to Leiden."

"Oh, Leiden. A sorry business, an awful mix-up—but I thought you said you saw her in Paris. Why didn't you ask her then?"

"Well, we never had a chance to speak because . . ."

"Because she had too much attention," he finished.

I nodded, glad he answered for me, relieved at not having to clarify I would have approached Maggie, but not Mata Hari.

Then he shuffled his chair a little closer to mine. He skimmed over Maggie's disgrace in Leiden, of which he seemed to know less than Mrs. Huizenga did. That he treated the thing as forgettable gave me some comfort. Then he told me about The Hague where she had answered an advertisement from an officer seeking marriage. He added that the officer, one Rudolf MacLeod, had returned from the Dutch East Indies, injured, and had presumably placed the advertisement to deal with his boredom. Maggie answered it and their engagement came only months later.

The idea of any woman, especially a lovely, spirited one such as Maggie resorting to such devices to find a husband would have been beyond my comprehension, had my cousin, Ingrid, not joked about it as well.

"Oh, it happens quite often," Zelle said, correctly guessing my thoughts. "I might not have known about her marriage except she was only nineteen then and they needed my written approval."

The cackling of several unruly teenagers riding past on bicycles distracted me and caused me to miss some of what he was saying. They were kicking a ball forward, fighting for it too, playing a mix of polo and football. The rudeness in their voices and the sound of the ball smacking against the walls was loud enough to bring out the proprietor to shake a fist at them. One of the children laughed at the poor man.

". . . but yes, I demanded from MacLeod that he present himself here, in a proper carriage, as was my due as her father and an important man. It hurt me when M'Greet took his side, but perhaps she was uncomfortable with my current humble situation. Nevertheless, I continued to insist, threatening not to sign the release, as was my right. Of course, I would have signed eventually, if that were what M'Greet truly wanted. But I had to meet the man first. It was my duty to find out what he was like."

"And what was he like?"

"Ah yes, I did meet him here, and they did come, as I had requested. Of course, then I demanded I attend the wedding. Chauffeured in a fine carriage. The illustrious father of such a beautiful bride—did you ever see my portrait painted before King Willem's visit?"

"Please, Mr. Zelle, can you tell me what he's like?"

"What is he like? An officer, from the east. They're all the same. Gruff, superior, boorish, lacking class. Good riddance."

The proprietor returned and, even though our glasses were still half-full, I signalled for two more beers. When they came, Zelle's demeanour, rather than cheering, turned morose. I tried to follow the stream of vitriol against his former son-in-law, the man's poor treatment of Maggie in the East Indies, the mysterious and tragic death of their son, Norman, his philandering, the beatings and insults, how he withheld money from her, and on and on.

"I could write a book," he said, going on to say none of it was exaggeration, that all his accusations were public record, recorded when Maggie filed for a divorce MacLeod did not contest. Nonetheless, it seemed unreal to me; I couldn't imagine Maggie allowing any of that to happen. Then again, I could never have imagined seeing her in Paris . . .

"They are divorced then?" I said. "You must be pleased about that."

"Yes, very pleased, except for Nonnie, my granddaughter."

He explained the girl, Jeanne-Louise, born seven years ago, not long after the MacLeods' arrival in the Indies, now lived with the father, despite Maggie having won custody of her in the divorce.

"Giving her up was the hardest thing she ever did, but it was also the only way my dear daughter could move to Paris," Zelle said, with a resigned, calm tone. "It's so sad the choices one has to make in life at times."

"Well, you must agree that Amsterdam's a better environment for a young girl to grow up in than Paris," I said, nonchalantly.

That angry spark in his eyes returned, and in them, a layer of spite overtop a sea of pride. He raised his voice and leaned forward, almost knocking over his glass of beer.

"How dare you? You call yourself M'Greet's friend and then besmirch her. She is a wonderful mother."

"I didn't mean—"

"You see now, don't you, how unfair it is for you to come here and judge my daughter, and therefore judge me. It's not easy raising—do you have children, sir?"

About to say I had already told him so, I remembered Antje's name was the same as this man's dead wife and Maggie's mother. Fearing the potential confusion, I shrugged.

"Then I suggest you refrain from judging others. I, for one, have learned never to judge.

Others judge, and have judged me severely, prejudicially, and wrongly all my life. Whatever you've gathered from our discussion, whatever you decide to publish, do not judge me."

I decided to leave then, without correcting him. But I did want to judge him and blame him for Maggie becoming Mata Hari. Not only had he tolerated her ways, he seemed proud, even opportunistic, seeing personal gain from her notoriety. Such a mind would have an indirect, yet potent, influence on a poor child from her earliest years. Especially if that daughter was as devoted to her father as Maggie had been.

I found comfort in knowing it had nothing to do with my life. Adam Zelle, Maggie Zelle, Mata Hari, all of them were outside my control. Sad, but just the way it had to be.

When I reached my house and saw my little angel's face peeking out our window, I vowed to protect her diligently, no matter what it took, from all threats, to ensure she could lead, and would lead, a good life, a moral life. At the very least that meant disavowing and denying my connection with Maggie. And Mata Hari.

As it turned out, I was capable of doing much more than that.

The next day was the first Saturday in weeks I hadn't spent at the office. A refreshing rain in the morning had left the lawn verdant and the shrubs in our garden a glistening green in the afternoon. The tulips, roses, and hyacinths surrounding our grounds presented an array of bright colours. We were fortunate. Gardens had become a rarity in the city due to commercial development. Only the loudest of noises from inside our house or from the canal ever penetrated through to the back. Except for several twittering birds flying around the trees, and a rustling squirrel on the other side of the tall hedges, it was peacefully quiet.

Cornelia and I were sitting across from each other, a tea setting and plates of *Deventerkoek* and butter on the small table between us. Antje was still inside with Madeline who was giving our daughter a bath. The door leading out opened and I hoped it was her. Instead, it was Vincent, handing me a letter.

"I found this under a table," he said. "It must have fallen on the floor."

"It's Aunt Josephine," I said to Cornelia. Getting no response, I decided to read it aloud.

"'Dear nephew, you have been constantly on our minds since our surprising and wonderful reunion. Ingrid had hoped to hear from you earlier but I told her that, with your young family and your position in Amsterdam, you are far too busy to mind us. But I also fear some of what we discussed may have upset you. I hope that's not the case and that you share our desire to restore a bond between our families. In that spirit, I wish to invite you, your wife, and your adorable child to a little party to celebrate Ingrid's twenty-first birthday on 27 May.'"

I set the letter down, stood up to go inside.

"Where are you going?" Cornelia said.

"It's only a week away. We ought to respond to this immediately."

"Don't tell me you intend for us to go. It's too far."

"It's not that far."

"It is, if we bring Antje, and we would not go without Antje."

"Of course we'd take her," I said, in my most reasoning voice. "She's invited too. And I'll have you know it's actually a much shorter trip in terms of time there than to your parents' estate in Brielle. All in a single comfortable first-class coach from Centraal. No rough roads or horse and carriage transfers."

My wife stared at me, without answer, unable or unwilling to counter my logic. "To be honest, Wim, I have no desire to visit a provincial town, to spend time with—"

"With farmers?"

"You don't have to put it so coarsely. It's just not my—our world."

"Why? Because they're Frisians? You're starting to sound like my Opa—"

I stopped there, shocked at my readiness to say anything against my grandfather, a man I'd never criticized before, not even by implication.

"There you go again," she said, "putting words in my mouth. It's not your relatives, it's just—what on earth would we do there?"

"Isn't visiting family reason enough?" I said. "True, Leeuwarden is a small town, but it is as modern as any other. We won't catch the plague there. Not every trip needs to be about shopping or sites—although the dykes are fascinating— some trips can be just to visit. And there's also the matter that someday my cousin will go to America."

"I thought you said she had no money, or means, that it was just a dream."

"No, that's what my aunt thinks, not me," I said, before pausing and smiling with familial pride. "She's a determined girl."

To this, Cornelia said nothing. I then buttered another piece of the spiced cake and cut away the coating on each side the way my wife liked it before offering it to her. She declined and got up.

"Antje should be clean now."

I set the rejected cake down on the plate and watched my wife's slender frame gracefully retreat into the house. She would be twenty-five soon, three-and-a-half years my junior, but at times she behaved as if the gap was ten years.

A few minutes later, a door whisked open above me, compelling me to look up to the second floor terrace. Like a queen ready to address her subjects, Cornelia stood there, a clean and fresh Antje in her arms. I waved at them and my daughter's joyful expression once again trivialized an argument.

"Bring her down to the garden," I said.

My little girl was wearing her new powder-blue dress. I took her on my lap. My wife smiled when I tickled Antje under her chin to make her giggle. Then I broke off a piece of the cake I had cut for Cornelia and fed it to her. She ate it and stuck out her hands for another, and I obliged.

"Wim, don't give her too much, she'll become fat."

"Fine."

I gave her one more piece, and then finished the rest myself. When Antje clamoured for more, I showed her my empty hands. Remarkably, she seemed to accept this and nestled her tiny head into my chest. My wife's face brightened into a royal smile.

"I just had a brilliant idea," she said. "Let's invite them to my party."

"Invite who?" I said.

"The Terpstras."

"Oh," I said. "Oh," I said again, my voice rising agreeably. Her proposal was a good one. Especially for me. Every spring I dreaded the annual ordeal of being the sole Brink amongst dozens of van Rozebouts at Cornelia's birthday party. How nice it would be to have people around I could call my own.

"It shall be perfect," she said. "They can come to Amsterdam the day before and the five of us can go together from here. The party will give them a chance to see and meet people, different people. Who knows, your cousin might even meet a—"

"All right, I'm convinced," I said. "We can do that as well."

"As well as what?"

"As well as visit Leeuwarden."

"Why are you so insistent?"

"My aunt's been snubbed before by my family so I think she's sensitive."

"Oh, I'm sure she'll understand," Cornelia said, with a slight wave of her hand.

"I'm not. You've never met my aunt, so you don't know what she's like."

"And what is she like?"

"I suppose you'll have to go up north to find out," I said, with a grin.

"Don't be clever. It's not appealing to me when you *try* to be clever. And if, as you suppose, your aunt is offended, then why should I not be offended at that?"

"What?"

"Never mind. It'd be too much for all of us and I'm sure you're too busy at work too. Why are you so anxious to go back there again, anyway?"

"Listen, Cornelia," I said, an impulsive thought rushing to my mind, "what would you say if we were to visit America some day, when Antje is older and more independent, just the three of us?"

"What would I say?" she said, turning her head sharply to face me. "I'd say maybe I had better meet this cousin of yours."

"What are you talking about?"

"You know what." She paused to pick up my aunt's letter. "I must make sure Max invites Eric. An opportunity to advance her station."

"Advance? With LaPlante?" The loudness of my voice, laced with disgust caused Antje to start whimpering.

"Why not?" Cornelia said, taking our daughter and settling her into the crib.

It seemed useless to take this up further lest Cornelia turn proposal into mission. I retrieved some writing materials from inside and began composing a letter to my aunt, declining her invitation, and writing a counter-invitation. Cornelia read it and her eyes lit up.

"What do you want to change?" I said.

"Oh, don't look that way. Just add a postscript. It'll be a costume party—there you are again with that look—how protective you are of these people. I assure you they'll love it. Everyone loves a costume party."

"Not me," I said. "I have no costume ideas."

"You're resourceful. You'll come up with something. You always do."

Reluctantly, I assented, as I always did, and added the postscript. Perhaps it was a feeling of powerlessness that troubled me, my constant yielding to Cornelia's wishes. She was probably right in that the Terpstras would enjoy a costume party. In fact, I was certain Ingrid would embrace the idea, and my aunt would go along. I was the one who didn't care for it due mostly to the pressure of finding something to wear, and then feeling silly walking around all evening under a false persona. Antje stirred and I picked her up out of her crib, and held her until she settled down.

"You know, Cornelia, the party's going to be so busy. If we don't go up there, then Antje may never get to know her relatives on her father's side."

"They can come her the day before."

I supposed that answered my misgivings. Perhaps I wasn't giving Cornelia enough credit. From her perspective, from one who hadn't met these people, she was taking a risk in inviting them to her party, introducing these strangers to her family. Yet it still didn't seem to be enough, at least not for me.

"I might still go to Leeuwarden," I said.

"When would you propose to do that?"

"Next week, of course, for the twenty-seventh, the date of the invitation."

Cornelia ate a piece of cake and looked thoughtful but said nothing.

A loud bang, followed by a rumbling, mechanical sound broke the garden calm. The sound repeated, louder each time, and seemed to come from inside the house. I handed Antje to Cornelia and rushed inside, only to discover the servants gawking at something through the front windows. Cornelia and Antje came up behind me and together we looked out the door just opened by Vincent.

"Hello sister, hello brother-in-law, hello my beautiful, impish niece," Max called out, above the noisy engine sputtering off.

A small crowd of neighbours and passers-by had gathered around the horseless vehicle, no doubt the first many had seen up close. An odd contraption, square-shaped but populated with circular appendages. The bulbous headlights looked like a pair of binoculars while the horn was large enough to have come from an orchestra. The large, white steering wheel could have navigated a small ship.

Max turned away to answer a question from a bystander who was pointing at the hood. Max opened it to give him a quick look before closing it. Then he ambled up the steps toward us. Antje squirmed, somewhat confused at the face, which was unshaven and half-hidden behind a pair of goggles. She let out a squeal of delight when Max removed the eyewear. Despite my misgivings about my brother-in-law, not even I could begrudge my daughter's infantile infatuation with her uncle, which tended to bring out the best in Max.

After a handshake for me and a kiss for his sister, he took Antje in his hands and beckoned Cornelia to join him in the front seat. As she did, he squeezed the horn, causing a bleating sound to emanate from the car. Cornelia jumped and then laughed. Then Max asked me to climb in the back but I declined.

"Not going far, I hope," I said.

"Just around the corner there's a spot where I can leave it overnight."

They drove off and I went back into the house. I instructed Vincent to delay dinner for one hour, to add one more setting, and to bring some beer outside for us. Then I asked Madeline to prepare the guest room. A few minutes later, the three adventurers joined me in the garden.

"Where on earth did you get that?" I asked.

"A birthday present from mom and dad," Max said, and then winked at his sister.

"You think they'll get me one for my birthday?" Cornelia said.

I looked at her and frowned. "We don't need a motorcar in Amsterdam. Where would we keep it?"

Cornelia shrugged, as if those were insignificant details.

"Actually," Max said, "this car is for all of us to share."

"You don't drive that around in Paris, do you?" I said.

"No, the car stays at the estate in Brielle, for driving around the countryside. Father just let me take it here to show you. He expects it back tomorrow afternoon."

"Are the roads in good enough condition near the estate?" I said.

"Most are okay, in good weather, but some are very rough."

"What about petrol? How easy is it to get?"

"Not as difficult as you might think."

Cornelia was growing bored of our talk. Antje, meanwhile, followed the exchange like a tennis match. Max and I continued to talk about the mechanics of the car, enjoying a few more glasses of beer, while Cornelia's mind seemed to drift away as she drank her wine. Spirited by the alcohol, my wife interrupted to ask Max to teach her to drive it. He looked at his glass of beer and then the darkening sky.

"Not now I hope. Unless I'm mistaken, the car doesn't work so well in the canal."

"What about tomorrow morning?" she said.

"Tomorrow is Sunday, and we have church," I said.

"Church?" Max said, bemused.

"Yes, church," I said, firmly.

"Ever since his trip to Marseille, Wim's adopted the strictness of his grandfather, Geert. We must go every week now. What did you to do to him in Paris, Max?" My brother-in-law and I exchanged glances. "Oh Wim, we can skip church this one time," Cornelia said.

I slowly shook my head but couldn't tell if she noticed my reaction. It had been getting progressively darker outside, the few bright stars in the sky providing only dim illumination for us.

I was about to voice my objection but then a servant interrupted to light several candles and the gaslight by the entrance to the house. When she left, Cornelia turned to me, her face all of a sudden fierce.

"Antje and I *will be* going for a drive tomorrow morning."

"As long as it's early and you bring our daughter back in time for church," I said, evenly. We stared at each other and my inner calmness surprised me during that drawn-out moment.

"I don't mind rising early," Max said.

"Good, then you can join us at church too," I said, to lighten the mood. To his credit, my brother-in-law smiled.

"Oh, Max, I haven't told you the delightful news yet," Cornelia said, her face glowing. "My party will have a new guest of honour this year."

"You mean Eric has been displaced?" Max said.

"Guest of honour?" I said.

"Yes, Wim, I'm making Ingrid my guest of honour. This will be the best way for her to get to know our people."

"Our people?" I said.

"Who is Ingrid?" Max said, indifferently.

"Ingrid Terpstra is Wim's long lost cousin from Leeuwarden whom he discovered right after he came home from Marseille when his uncle sadly passed away."

"Leeuwarden, eh?" Max said, giving me a long look.

I nodded slowly but uneasily. I didn't care for this reminder that I had not told my wife anything about Mata Hari, never mind the dancer's link with Leeuwarden. In my wife's mind, I had only gone north for Uncle Dick. Cornelia shifted in her seat and now seemed to sense something between Max and me. Her ignorance indicated to me her brother had kept his word and told his sister nothing about Paris.

"Wim grew up there, remember?" she said, unwilling to let the topic drop for some reason.

"You're right, I had forgotten. Wim so rarely talks about his youth. Although recently—"

I coughed and he stopped.

"That's just it. Wim's hardly ever mentioned them before and now, all of a sudden, he and his aunt and cousin are the best of relations."

Vincent came outside to inform us dinner was almost ready. We followed him inside, Max and I to the dining room where we took our seats, while Cornelia saw Antje to bed. I asked Vincent to open some wine.

"While on your family visit, did you happen to look up any old friends?" Max whispered, conspiratorially.

"Drop it," I said. "It's a dead issue."

"Do you mean to declare she wasn't your old friend, after all?"

His tone troubled me. I felt an urge to ask if he had talked to Mata Hari since that time, except doing so might expose more than I wanted.

"Precisely," I said.

"Relax, I haven't told anyone in the family about what happened in Paris."

"Thank you." A moment passed. "Why not?"

"To be honest," he said, with a chuckle, "I've developed a sort of addiction to your dancing friend, one I'd prefer to keep to myself."

"She's not my—what?" I said.

"Of course, of course, she's not your friend. Which is good, because then it should be of no consequence to admit this to you. Man to man. I've become positively captivated by Mata Hari, enraptured, bewitched, spellbound—"

"Max."

"Yes, sorry. My point is I rarely miss a performance. I keep trying to meet her but it's nearly impossible. Not even Eric with his credentials—but let me clear one thing up before you start. I'm not in love with her in the way so many others are. I'm content to watch her perform."

Had he shared this detail to appease me, or to test me? Either way, I had to be on guard for I was committed to feigning ignorance about the matter. Focusing on that helped quell the resentment I felt for Max who in my eyes was just another Bart Postma, one of thousands by now.

"So, tell me more about this cousin of yours. Ingrid Terpstra sounds charming. But then, I'm sure you think all the girls from Leeuwarden—"

"She is charming, Max, but Cornelia's never met her. And Ingrid is not like us, she is pure and innocent, so if you do one thing for me, please leave her alone."

My brother-in-law seemed taken aback, perhaps even hurt, but he nodded assent. A bit too quickly, I thought, and I wasn't sure I could trust him. Cornelia then joined us at the table just as our soups came.

"Your husband is protective of his cousin," Max said, as we walked.

Cornelia, after consuming half the bowl, took the spoon from her mouth and grinned.

"I suspect, from what I hear, the little cousin has bewitched your poor sister's husband."

I sighed but deemed the remark otherwise unworthy of a response.

"Of course, it could always be the other way around," Max said.

"Max, dear brother, I want you to instruct Eric to intervene on my behalf at my party, to entertain the young lady."

I couldn't tell if she was still joking. For the rest of the night, I tried to get Max alone to emphasize my wish for him to leave Ingrid alone extended to his friends too, particularly Eric, but without success. After dinner, we retired to the front sitting room.

As they talked, reliving childhood memories I had heard dozens of times before, laughing and sharing a few glasses of wine, I sat back in the large wingback chair, wondering about Antje who, like me, was an only child. Perhaps she might benefit by having a younger brother too. However, considering Antje's long and difficult birth, I doubted Cornelia would want to brave that again. But one never knew.

When their reminiscences began to include Eric, I announced I was retiring for the night.

"Sleep well," Max said.

"Thank you. And Cornelia, if you and Max do go for a drive tomorrow, and especially if you intend on learning to drive, I want you to leave Antje here, with me."

"We'll see," she said.

The house was quiet. Disquietingly so. The guest room was empty, its bed already made. My wife's bedroom door was open and I saw Madeline tidying up. She informed me Cornelia had left instructions to wake her and Max just before dawn.

"I see, and what about my daughter?"

"With your wife and her brother, sir."

I found Vincent and told him I would take my breakfast in the garden. After finishing my hard-boiled egg, pancakes and grapefruit, I sat back with my coffee. They had left early and may not have gone far. There was still time, if they arrived soon, for the three of us to attend church together. Max could even drive us there, saving time.

But as the minutes passed, I became aware of a slow and dark emotion simmering inside me. It wasn't anger, but rather disappointment. Sprinkled with anger. Some of it was directed at myself for even thinking Cornelia might ever consider sacrificing her frivolity to my wishes. Such wilfulness can be an appealing, even beguiling, trait in a woman before marriage. However, once the vows are stated it ought to recede, without disappearing altogether.

At church, I took a wide position to try and reserve room on either side of me on the pew, just in case. Soon people on both sides began to encroach on my space and I couldn't stop them. In symbolic defiance, I did manage to keep empty a small portion, but one large enough for my daughter to have filled.

And I imagined her sitting next to me, bored and fidgeting but otherwise polite, as I listened ardently while Reverend Schultens spoke on the decline of modern society and on how all of us Christians share a measure of moral obligation. Only a measure, he emphasized; fight battles, not wars. It was not our personal responsibility to attempt defeating, single-handedly, such decline as a whole, but to do so in bits and pieces, using the means and individual gifts granted us by God. In his stirring sermon, he even cited Paris as a salvageable Gomorrah.

My brother-in-law was long on his way to return the car to Brielle when I returned home and found Cornelia with Antje in the garden. My wife's chastened demeanour neutralized my impulse to lecture. I picked up my daughter and we played on the grass for a little while, Cornelia watching us with a forlorn expression.

"What's the matter?" I finally said to her.

"You know, Wim, if you really wish to go to Leeuwarden, we can go, the three of us."

I stared at Cornelia, not sure I'd heard right. I couldn't recall a single instant in our lives when Cornelia had reversed her position on anything so unexpectedly.

"Did Max say something to make you change your mind?"

Cornelia looked confused, a little irritated too, but then shook her head. "What possibly could Max have to do with it?"

"I don't know," I said, in a coaxing way.

But something innocently genuine in her expression disarmed me. I distracted Antje with a toy so I could sit next to my wife.

"Max hasn't told you anything?" I said.

"Told me anything about what?"

I then related what happened in Paris, the full story, including how my recognition of Mata Hari had driven me to Leeuwarden as much as the death announcement had. Cornelia's face remained ambiguously sombre as she took this in and it felt good to get it off my mind. But when I finished, she began laughing. Not a mocking laugh, but rather the kind she used whenever Antje did something naughty. Such as pinching. My daughter interrupted her playing to watch us, with keen interest.

"Oh, it's all rather preposterous, don't you think?" Cornelia said, light-heartedly.

This was not at all the reaction I expected, which only exposed my ignorance of what I might have expected. Prior to this moment, I was sure Cornelia would have thought it low of me to attend such a performance. And then to find out I once might have known such an individual; I expected censure, not amusement. Her smile and the velvety tone of her voice were infectious and I couldn't help but join her in smiling when she put her hand on my shoulder with a tender touch. Inside, though, my stomach rumbled with confusion.

"So is she the girl you remembered?" she said.

"No," I said, looking away, toward Antje.

The lie came instantly and easily. I did want to tell Cornelia about Maggie but something in her look directed me to deny it and deny it emphatically. The instinct was so overpowering I gave no thought to the possibility there might be repercussions in the future. I wanted to avoid looking at her, out of shame for my deceit, but I had to, to see if she believed it. Nothing in her lovely face showed any sign of suspicion; instead, she began chuckling again.

"I wish I could have seen your face in Paris."

"I see. That amuses you, does it?"

"Sorry, but yes it does. Max should have known better."

"Yes, but that's not the point, is it?" I said.

"Why? What do you mean?"

"What I mean is . . . were you sincere about going to Leeuwarden?"

Cornelia nodded and then grinned. "Someday, after we see Paris. I want to see firsthand what the fuss is about this dancer."

"That could take forever," I said, choosing to ignore the reference to Mata Hari, "considering all the work at the office."

"Fret not, my dear husband, things often occur faster than we expect."

Ingrid

My cousin was one of the first passengers off
the train at Centraal Station. She was wearing
the same blue dress she wore on my second day
in Leeuwarden, when I came for dinner, the
only alteration a silk bonnet. We embraced. She
allowed me to take her suitcase but insisted on
holding on to an intricately arranged bouquet of
flowers and a square box. I led her out into the
unusually warm, but cloudy June day.

"Welcome to Amsterdam," I said, grandly
describing a circle along the Prins Hendrikaade,
from the Schreierstoren—the Tower of Tears
where sad wives used to cry goodbyes to
departing sailors—to the Haarlemmeerweg.

"I have been to Amsterdam before."

"Of course," I said, assuming her response
meant to save me the effort rather than express
impatience. I hailed a cab.

The cobbled roadway of the Damrak was
hectic with horses, coaches, and one or two
backfiring motorcars, the pedestrian lanes
clogged with luggage-bound tourists seeking

hotels, indecisive ones choosing boats for canal tours, and entrepreneurs aiming to fulfill those needs, at exorbitant profit.

"But that building's new," Ingrid said.

She was pointing at a modern structure occupying a full block along Amsterdam's busiest street. It stood out because of its ornate arched entrances, asymmetrically placed towers, and windows of various sizes and shapes. Concrete friezes and statues sculpted into the pillars added an artistic element but the building clearly had been designed to serve a functional purpose. Her interest delighted me.

"Why that's the exchange," I said, "the Beurs van Berlage. It's where I work. I like how it reminds me of the Grote Kerk in Leeuwarden."

"Oh," she said, "I suppose, in a way."

I guessed she was nervous about meeting Cornelia. Perhaps she was sore we hadn't come for her birthday. Especially as work had been my excuse, and here I was reminding her of it, boasting no less. Past the Dam monument and the Royal Palace, the cab's pace quickened on the less congested Rokin and soon the Munttoren came into view. From there a short curving ride alongside the Amstel River brought us to the Herengracht.

Our three-storey house, with its three narrow but tall windows, fit snugly between two others of similar size and design. Like all the canal houses, ours leaned slightly toward the waterway, along which moored a long row of houseboats. The brick was a pinkish red with door and window trims freshly painted dark green.

"I always dreamed of living in one of these," Ingrid said, this time unreservedly impressed.

"Well, tonight you shall," I said, as I led her inside.

After presenting the bouquet of flowers to Cornelia—yellow carnations mixed with some pink roses—Ingrid dug through her small suitcase until she found a knitted puppy. Antje adored her gift and clutched it tightly. However, my daughter abandoned the puppy when Ingrid produced a pair of little dolls, a boy and a girl dressed in traditional Frisian costumes. These promised to be Antje's favourites for a long time.

"This is the outfit worn by the women in my mother's village, north of Leeuwarden," Ingrid said, to Antje. "Many still wear them now."

My daughter seemed to understand. She looked up at this newcomer, regarding her with interest, before focusing on the toy, which she touched gently.

"You made it yourself?" Cornelia said, her tone full of admiration, no trace of contempt.

"Not the doll, but I did sew the clothing."

"I see," Cornelia said, nodding.

The way my wife kept smelling the flowers showed her first impression of my cousin was a positive one. The feeling appeared mutual too by the way Ingrid nodded humbly back. Indeed, everything was going far better than I could have hoped. Then Ingrid pulled out a small bottle of *Oude Jenever* for me, an expensive brand I hadn't tried yet.

"Thank you," I said. "But gifts like this will only delay your American dreams."

"Oh no, it's from my mother. But I did bring something else for you."

She then handed me the box she had not let me carry and motioned for me to open it. Inside, wrapped in tissue paper and neatly folded, my father's Zouave uniform. I pulled it out, held it up. A lingering odour of mothballs was evident but not oppressive, as if someone had made an effort to air it out. It seemed sturdier too, as if recently mended in places.

"Funny," I said, "I've been thinking about this a lot lately."

"It's been gathering dust in our attic," Ingrid said. "My mother took it when . . . well, she feared your grandfather might have destroyed it otherwise."

"Thank you," I said.

"We would have given it to you last month, if you could have come."

"I'm so sorry about that," I said. "I—we—"

"Oh no," Ingrid said, alarmed, "I didn't mean to criticize."

"Well, Wim, it appears now you have a costume for my party, after all," Cornelia said.

"You can't be serious," I said. "It still smells slightly and I doubt it will fit."

"I can't smell it and we'll all be outside. As far as size, just give it to Vincent. He can arrange alterations tonight. At least let him try."

"I suppose," I said, now enjoying a rush of relief at solving a vexing problem.

"Now let's get you settled," my wife said, whisking my cousin aside.

She waved for Madeline to take Ingrid's bag upstairs, and then beckoned Ingrid to follow.

Apprehension returned to me over Cornelia's impending inspection of Ingrid's attire prior to our departure for Brielle. At least my wife had been kind enough to warn me she would do this.

They were upstairs at least half an hour but came back with big smiles. I knew Cornelia well enough to distinguish her polite smiles of obligation from her sincere ones. This was one of the latter and, in fact, one of the cheeriest expressions I'd seen on my wife for some time. Then I noticed that Ingrid had changed out of her dress into one of my wife's smart black skirts with matching tan blouse. A bit snug on my cousin but fine otherwise.

"I think we're ready for a leisurely stroll along the canals," I said.

"That can wait, Wim, we have other pressing matters."

"Cornelia wants to take me shopping," Ingrid said, with childlike glee, all traces of her nervousness gone.

Cornelia's glance confirmed she had found my cousin's clothes wanting. While her audacity annoyed me, I had to admit it pleased me to see my wife show such sisterly concern for my cousin. Ensuring Ingrid's appearance was up to van Rozebout standards was as much in my cousin's interest as in my wife's, perhaps more. Then Ingrid let out a yelp as she jumped away from Antje.

"Did she just pinch me?" Ingrid said, chuckling through a grimace.

"Antje," Cornelia said, unable to hold back a grin. "I'm sorry, she's been doing that lately."

"Never to me," I said.

"That's not true and you know it. Do you mind entertaining the little skin squeezer while we shop?"

"No reason for Antje and me not to come along at least part of the way," I said.

"Oh, that reminds me, there's a letter from America for you."

"America?" Ingrid said, but then Cornelia gave my cousin a gentle push into the hallway.

My exclusion annoyed me until I watched them descend the stairs outside. Then I chided myself for my selfishness. I ought to have been pleased at seeing my wife and Ingrid so quickly taking to each other. A little lost time with my cousin was a small investment for that kind of harmony. Meanwhile, the letter would provide a distraction. Because it was from Mark Dekker.

In exchanging contact cards at the dykes, Mark and I did so as people often do, politely but with only a vague expectation of following up. But after Ingrid's announcement of her American intentions, I asked myself, why not forge a connection with someone overseas in case those dreams materialized? So I sent him a letter. And sure enough, here was a reply. Ah, if only he were still in Europe; I'd have had no qualms about inviting him to join us at my wife's party.

Mark wrote he was pleased to hear from me and that he hoped to maintain contact. He reaffirmed his earlier claim that there was no shortage of opportunities in Boston, and in all of America, and that he'd be happy to help my cousin should the occasion arise.

Cornelia and Ingrid returned from their shopping barely in time for supper, brimming with secret excitement, several bags of bounty in their hands. A hearty meal of beef tenderloin with vegetables and red wine ensured a good night's rest ahead of us. Though anxious to tell Ingrid about Mark's letter, I determined it was not my place to interfere this way. At least not yet, not before I had consulted with her mother.

My cousin retired first. I was ready to do so as well but then my wife pulled me to the garden. Sparse but rapidly moving clouds alternately hid and revealed a myriad of stars. A mixed meteorological omen for tomorrow's journey to Brielle.

"Your cousin is wonderful," Cornelia said.

"Especially now that you've clothed her."

"Yes, and thank you for allowing me to do so without a lecture. Her clothes were horrid. But no longer. In fact, I bought her so many things I also had to get her something to carry them back in."

"Oh Cornelia, I hope you never spoil Antje like that."

"I won't if you don't," she said.

"Funny. I'm sure Ingrid appreciates it, and I do too," I said. "I really do."

"You know, now I feel badly we missed her birthday. That was selfish of me. I hope this makes up for it."

I sat up. It wasn't in Cornelia's nature to apologize. And this only a few weeks after her about face regarding us visiting Leeuwarden. Something had changed with my wife but I couldn't pin down what it might be. I decided to take her words at face value and enjoy this moment of mutual warmth and compatibility.

"So where did you two go shopping? What did you talk about?"

"Oh we covered such a lot, and that goes for both questions. And yes, before you ask, I made sure we avoided the Kalverstraat until after four o'clock."

"I'm glad to hear it."

"I should say your description of your cousin was not at all flattering enough, and more than a little misleading."

"How do you mean?"

"You told me she was cordial and sweet and generous and all kinds of sentimental things. You never mentioned her good looks and strong will. She acted at ease in even the finest shops."

"I never said she wouldn't," I said.

"But you implied it."

"Not at all, Cornelia. Those perceptions were only your prejudices."

She did not argue this point, which made me feel somewhat victorious.

I can still recall an incident that took place in 1890. I was thirteen and it was only days after my moving to Amsterdam to live with my grandparents. I had nearly finished my plate at dinner when a sombre, liveried servant loomed over me, frowning slightly. Only I didn't know he was a servant; I thought he was a guest, a guest displeased with me for some reason. In Leewuarden, I would have ignored him, or told him in some unkind way to leave me alone. But in Amsterdam, somewhat intimidated by a gruff grandfather I was still getting to know, my confidence abandoned me. I meekly asked the man what I was doing wrong, addressing him as, sir. He just stood there, his stony face expressing nothing. Laughter from Oma Isabelle added to my confusion and distress. I didn't catch on until Opa Geert explained the man was a servant—Vincent, the same Vincent who was working for me then in 1905 but who has passed on since—and that he had only been waiting to take my plate and ask what I wanted for dessert.

Ingrid reminded me of that the next day at Centraal Station. As we were about to board the train, she followed Madeline and another servant to the second-class carriage. Cornelia and I shared a brief chuckle, letting her almost get on before calling her back. My blushing cousin returned and took the seat reserved for her next to the window demurely. I shared my anecdote, which Cornelia found droll but Ingrid thought amusing.

My wife and daughter began dozing once the buildings and avenues gave way to green countryside and dirt paths, muddied by the thunderstorm the night before. Although Ingrid engaged me in conversation, her detached manner was nothing like the effusiveness she had shown in Leeuwarden, or even the day before with Cornelia.

"It's unfortunate your mother couldn't join us," I said.

"The travel would have been too much."

"I hope it didn't upset her that we couldn't attend your birthday."

"She understands, as do I. Besides, Cornelia has vowed the three of you will visit her in Leeuwarden before the summer is out."

"Has she?" I said, glancing at my wife whose eyes had opened slightly but then shut again. Something in what Ingrid said troubled me but I couldn't put my finger on it. "Are you enjoying yourself so far?"

"Oh yes. Cornelia has been so sweet to me, so generous. What wonderful taste she has."

"You enjoyed your shopping, that's good."

"Not just the shopping, Wim, but the friendship. I don't have brothers or sisters and, well, to be honest, not many friends either."

A conductor came by to punch our tickets, which should not have happened as they had been punched just after we'd boarded. Ingrid, instead of nervously obliging as I expected her to do, diplomatically chastised the man for his error. His face turned red and he apologized. Ingrid then instructed him to prepare a pot of tea and have it delivered to our compartment, along with three cups.

"Right away ma'am." the man said, ceremoniously doffing his cap before continuing on.

"I hope I didn't offend him," Ingrid said. "He won't be mad, will he?"

"Not at all," I said, chuckling, now feeling far less concerned about her ability to manage herself with the van Rozebouts than I had the day before. "By the way, how are your plans for the United States going?"

"Fine," she said, in an odd way and with a low voice. "Splendid, actually," Ingrid then added, as if aware of her unresponsiveness.

"Does that mean you've made progress?"

"Yes, I have made progress."

"Well?"

"Do you mind if we discuss it later?" she said, almost whispering now, as if not wanting my wife to hear. I could only conclude she was willing to talk, but hoped to do so in private. The tea came shortly and Ingrid poured out two cups—Cornelia was sleeping fully now—which we drank in silence.

A carriage was waiting at Rotterdam to take us on the second half of the journey. My wife arranged the seats so she and Ingrid could face forward, allowing Cornelia to point out the landmarks along the way, while I held Antje next to me, opposite them. I also needed to monitor our physical well-being once we got going and the carriage began rocking side to side. My attention turned to anxiety when our skittish horses resisted the approach to the ferry that would transport us across the Maas. A new steel bridge at Spijkenisse had opened two years before—it still reminds me of the bridges in New York—but we had decided to take the traditional route via Vlaardingen because of Cornelia's fear of heights.

Now I regretted that decision, more so when I smelled ale on the coachman's breath. As the ferry rocked in the wake of several barges, I stared at the giant metal span in the distance, nursing regret into irritation. The horses once again became agitated at the other side. I decided to risk the delay, along with Cornelia's chagrin, and change them. I also found and hired a new coachman. This meant a wait of half an hour, as well as a further delay to change horses before Brielle. I just didn't want to take any more chances with these animals.

Alas, the muddy roads proved awfully slow going for the poor beasts. My fellow passengers didn't seem to notice. Antje stayed asleep while her mother joyfully took in the surroundings, occasionally waving at someone in a field and then explaining who it was to Ingrid. My cousin alternated her attention to the wide sweeps of green fields and pasture and the arrays of livestock on our left and the mounds of dykes blocking the Maas from view to our right. She pointed out a cluster of buildings on a hilltop; they reminded her of the *terpen* in Friesland. Occasionally, we would see puffs and billows of smoke, in various shades of grey, evidence of steamers headed into port or out to sea.

"I imagine they're like the signals American Indians send from fires on the plains," she said.

"You know about American Indians," I said.

"I've read a great deal," she said, but chose not to elaborate.

The usual feeling of trepidation came over me upon our approach to a pair of wide and tall wrought iron gates, each topped by a stylized, encircled "vR." The domain of my in-laws was a distinct world, as distinct from my world as Europe from America, Paris from Leeuwarden. An electric motor, installed since the last time we were there, opened the gates automatically to let us in.

Thick hedges, twelve feet high, combined with the giant oak and maple trees to guard the property's perimeter, blocking out evidence of neighbours. Two columns of new birch trees planted several years ago flanked the long dirt path leading to the estate entrance. They were maturing nicely, the leaves from their thin but sturdy branches occasionally thwacking against the carriage's windows. In future summers, those new trees would obscure much of the grounds, including the marshy pond in its centre, from incoming visitors. An effect I knew the van Rozebouts desired, for privacy reasons; however, I feared it would make the approach to the estate entrance seem a doomed journey.

Labelling the van Rozebout country home a large house or a small mansion was debatable; its ornamentations were grandiose, but the building's compact size ensured it did not feel imposing. The whiteness of the stone and the symmetry of its design, a lowlands variation on English Tudor, particularly appealed to me.

"Marvellous," Ingrid said.

"This is where I grew up," Cornelia said.

My wife then asked the driver to take the trail that circumnavigated the pond. Each of the surrounding benches had been adorned with birthday decorations. The carriage then drove up the semi-circle driveway where it stopped in front of Cornelia's waiting father and mother.

It was hard to tell which parent Cornelia took after more; her physical and facial features seemed to inherit equally from both. The average height, white skin, blonde hair, small nose, and intense eyes were most evident in her mother while the slender but firm build, soft chin and long neck clearly came from her father. Her wild laughs, wild expressions, and demonstrative arm movements were all her own invention, a sharp contrast to her parents' reserved countenances.

Cornelia's father whispered an instruction to Jacob—the family's personable major-domo for thirty years—who took a restless Antje, into the house to her play area. Cornelia's father then helped the two ladies down and introduced Mrs. van Rozebout and himself to Ingrid.

"Queenie!" Cornelia said, her face alit, as she bolted inside.

She returned cradling a large, fluffy, orange and white cat with a brown mark on its nose. A rambunctious outdoor feline, and a predator. Cornelia had had to leave Queenie behind when we moved into our house in Amsterdam.

"Careful, dear, don't let her loose, she's still recovering," Cornelia's mother said.

"Recovering?" my wife said, alarmed. "From what?"

As an answer, a much smaller version of the cat, followed by two others met us at the door. Unlike Queenie's fine pedigree coat, little clumps and small black spots marred the colouring in the kittens' furs. Cornelia's mother tried to shoo them back inside the house, until a servant came to her aid.

"What a nuisance," Mrs. van Rozebout said. "It's been hard finding homes for these things."

Ingrid then picked one up and petted it, causing it to purr rapidly.

"We're not keeping them?"

Cornelia's question drew instant headshakes from her parents. She then cast a look of appeal at me, a melancholic echo of that sad little girl on the Willemskade.

"Absolutely not," I said. "Remember, Antje's allergic."

"Would you like one to take back with you, dear?" Mrs. van Rozebout said, to Ingrid.

"They are adorable," my cousin said. "But no, that would not be possible. It's so sad though, being taken away from your mother so young."

"That is the way of life sometimes," Mrs. van Rozebout said.

"I suppose," Ingrid said, and then handed the kitten to a servant.

"Of course it is, my dear. Especially if you know it will be better taken care of in the new environment, or taken care of at all."

"Mother," Cornelia said, in mock reproach.

We all laughed, except Ingrid, who was unaware of the family reference. While Cornelia had loved Queenie, she had struggled with the responsibility, forgetting to feed her, and then feeding her too much, not brushing her, leaving her out at night, and so on.

"These are such lovely grounds," my cousin said.

"Let me take you for a tour of the house," my father-in-law said, clearly pleased by the compliment and charmed by the source.

Ingrid took his arm and they went inside together, followed by my wife and her mother. I followed them only as far as the library, the ritual conclusion of the tour, as I recalled from my first visit. Jacob was kind enough to bring me a *borrel* and then to leave me alone.

I closed my eyes, happy for a few moments of privacy before the house and grounds would fill with guests. Perhaps it would be different this time, with Ingrid here. I had to admit I was curious about her reactions and interactions, particularly with Max and Eric. A good twenty minutes of blissful peace passed before I heard people approaching.

"What a wonderful portrait!" My cousin's exclamation startled me. I turned to see her standing with Cornelia, their faces drawn to the wall behind me, above the fireplace. "It looks like a Rembrandt," Ingrid added.

"It does, doesn't it?" Cornelia said.

"It's not?" Ingrid said.

"Not unless my lovely daughter will be turning three hundred something tomorrow," Cornelia's father said, upon entering the room.

"That's you?" Ingrid said, turning to Cornelia. No one answered and I watched my cousin as her head switched back and forth between the wall at which I didn't care to look and my wife. "Oh my goodness, it is indeed."

They were discussing the painting of a very young Cornelia, created by Max's friend, Eric LaPlante, when he was in art school. Long before I knew any of them. His instructor had challenged Eric and the class to copy a Rembrandt masterpiece. Eric had chosen the portrait of Cornelia Pronck, wife of Albert Cuyper. The coincidence in Christian names inspired the young artist to convince Cornelia van Rozebout to model for him. He wanted to create his own version, declaring he eschewed all forms of duplication. My future wife happened to own a black frock similar to the one worn by her namesake, and Eric found a broad lace collar and bonnet with frills like those worn in the seventeenth century. Cornelia had no difficulty looking lovely and elegant while posing, managing to affect a stern Mona Lisa-like expression. The instructor, though impressed by Eric's talent, nevertheless failed the student for not following direction. Eric abandoned painting forever then—or so he claimed—and had given the portrait as a gift to Cornelia for her twentieth birthday.

When I first saw it, I was captivated at how it revealed my wife's vibrancy. So much so, I couldn't help feeling envious toward the artist whose art seemed to betray a too intimate awareness of his subject. And when I finally met Eric, my feelings toward the painting changed. I hated it. I hated it because I was convinced his interest in Cornelia then—and since—went beyond posing. My wife always remained coy about those posing sessions, to avoid self-incrimination perhaps, or just to taunt me. Henceforth, I could never regard the painting without awareness of the artist, especially with the rather prominent swirls of the LaPlante signature in the bottom right.

"I was eighteen then, asked to pose by a . . . friend of the family," Cornelia said.

"By Eric LaPlante," I said. "It's okay, you can say his name."

Ingrid looked at me quizzically, almost as if unaware of my presence until that moment.

"Eric's someone we'll be sure to introduce you to later," Cornelia said, to Ingrid, as if he was someone famous. This drew a cough from her father. "Speaking of which, daddy, where is Max, and where is the car?"

Mr. van Rozebout took us to a window and pointed out to a large gardener's shed, an open wooden structure similar to a barn, only without doors. Wheelbarrows, shovels, and bags of soil, and other gardening paraphernalia lined the perimeter while in the middle stood an empty space, large enough for a motorcar, judging by the pattern of the wheel impressions on the ground.

"I'm afraid your brother is stranded in Rotterdam due to the rain from last night. The roads are barely passable for horses, let alone that contraption. Some roads are so bad I doubt they will clear in time for your brother to make it to the party. Eric too has sent his regrets."

"That's terrible," Cornelia said. She looked ready to cry. "I so wanted all of us to go to the beach at Rockanje on Sunday."

"Why would that stop us from going?" I said.

"It won't be the same without a car."

Cornelia then excused herself and left the room, followed by her father promising to see if he could do anything. I sat back down in the same chair with my back to the fireplace while Ingrid took the one opposite me.

"That portrait would look perfect in your front room, the one that looks out on the canal," she said.

"I prefer it here," I said, half-heartedly.

"You don't like it, do you?"

"It's a fine painting, masterful really. In fact, when I first laid eyes on it, it made me adore Cornelia that much more."

"I see. It's the painter you don't care for." I let my lack of denial answer for me. "You and Cornelia are so very different," Ingrid added, moments later, in a measured tone.

What it intended to measure, I couldn't say.

Costumed affairs always created a dilemma for an unimaginative businessman like me, and would have this time if not for Ingrid showing up with my father's Zouave uniform. I felt the same swell of pride putting it on as I had felt as a child watching my father do so on that special Sunday in Leeuwarden. First the stockings, then the trousers, the shirt, the shoes, and finally the red belt around my waist. I felt something else too, the childlike joy of dressing up as a soldier.

I had no trouble with the leggings and *jambiere* but the collarless coat was thick and felt heavy, not to mention large in the chest. I did up the buttons with care, before discovering Vincent, or Aunt Josephine or Ingrid, had thoughtfully double sewn them. The sash was a nuisance too but looked good. The red fez perfected the ensemble. Whilst staring at the mirror, which I had done for some time prior to coming outside, I couldn't help but imagine Maggie Zelle's reaction. "Smells like mothballs," she might have quipped, just to tease me, followed by something complimentary.

I stepped through a pair of French doors that opened on to a patio with several empty circular tables surrounded by chairs. Behind those, a long rectangular table, one-half dominated by a giant German chocolate cake, ringed by trays of *gebakjes* and other sweets, the other half stacked with plates and cutlery etched with the crest of a local caterer. Another table stood empty awaiting birthday gifts.

Cornelia's parents came out shortly after me, dressed as Napoleon Bonaparte and Josephine. I bowed in admiration at the fine detailing of their attire. Their daughter appeared moments later and stood beside them, her bosom too exposed to my liking, but no more so than at other times.

"Marie Antoinette," my wife said, cheerfully.

I was wondering whether I'd missed some memorandum dictating a French theme until my cousin came through the doors. Her bright face stood out like a doll, in fact, just like the doll she had brought for Antje.

A blue-and-white checked bonnet covered her head, with her blonde hair falling down in braids over her blouse of a matching blue-and-white checked pattern. Her skirt, traditional and modestly hemmed below the ankles, was dark grey, with a yellow and red trim at the bottom. The ensemble fit Ingrid well though I suspected it might have belonged to my aunt when she was younger and thinner. Ingrid was even wearing clogs. They made a terrible noise against the cobblestone patio although they would keep her feet dry on the marshy grass.

"Isn't she delightful?" Cornelia said.

"Yes, certainly," I said.

"But what on earth are you wearing, Wim?" my mother-in-law said.

"Don't you think it's fabulous?" Cornelia said, while Ingrid nodded. "It's the uniform his father wore while fighting in the Civil War. You can even see the wound marks."

"Oh my," my mother-in-law said, more in awe than shock. My father-in-law showed no reaction.

A rumble of horses proclaimed the first guests, Cornelia's cousin, Edward, and his wife, Justine. He came dressed as a Musketeer and she as Joan of Arc. We barely had time to introduce Ingrid before more guests were announced, launching an invasion of uncles, aunts, cousins, grandparents, friends, and business acquaintances. Characters from French history inspired most of the costumes, although I did spot an American Indian, a Genghis Khan, and several explorers. Drinks were distributed, cliques formed and dispersed, and the party was underway.

"Have you noticed," Ingrid said, taking me aside at one point, "that all the guests, except you and I, are wearing costumes of people they can never be?"

"How so?"

"You can be a soldier. I can be a village girl. But that man over there, he can never be Christopher Columbus."

"Very perceptive," I said, after looking around and seeing she was right, although unsure what her observation meant to signify. "And you're proving to be quite popular."

"Stop. You'll make me blush."

"Ingrid, come join us over here," called out a young lady ten yards away.

"Do you mind, Wim?"

"By all means."

My cousin's ability to flit from group to group, disengaging and engaging with poise, amazed me. Her costume was seen as ironic and everyone treated her as an elegant and modern woman rather than the provincial girl I had only begun to know. I felt more at ease now.

My association with Ingrid seemed to have improved my popularity too. Whereas on previous gatherings I tended to hang back and listen, people now involved me in weighty discussions, seeking my views on Albert Einstein and the theories he had published a few weeks earlier; speculations on when the Russo-Japanese War might end; fears that continuing advances in weaponry would spawn unimaginable casualties in future wars—sadly a too accurate prediction—and the general distress over the recent tragic earthquake that had killed twenty thousand in India.

The advent of technology was a dominant theme. In due course, we covered the prospects for the motorcar, the steamship, electricity, and more. Yet not all topics were so grave or scientific. In one discussion, I predicted my football team, Ajax of Amsterdam, would someday surpass the local favourite, Sparta Rotterdam, as the best in all of Holland. That prediction drew mostly good-natured sneers.

Things were going well until Cornelia's quirky giggle interrupted my debate about transatlantic steamship speed records with two of her uncles. The sound came from a barely lit patch of field beyond the pond near the woods.

There stood Ingrid and my wife amidst a group of her cousins and their friends, all young, all male, all eligible bachelors, all with morals closer to Max's than mine. The smiles, the gay laughter, the plumes of cigarette smoke: this was precisely the type of scenario I had feared. I excused myself and hastened there but Cornelia intercepted me. When I tried to pass, she steered me toward the house.

"Where are you off to, dear husband?"

"You oughtn't to leave Ingrid there, by herself, with those men."

"Come with me. My father wants us."

"You go on. I'd rather stay here."

Cornelia chuckled, shrugged her shoulders, and walked off. When I looked over there again, the smoke had gone and that conversation had broken up. I now found Ingrid with two older ladies, Cornelia's spinster aunts, her mother's older twin sisters.

". . . all the way to the United States of America?" Aunt Anneke was saying to Ingrid.

"Yes, why not?" my cousin said, in a tone less of defiance than pride.

"Lovely and innocent young women such as you ought not to travel alone, in my humble opinion," Aunt Inneke added.

How strange. Earlier my cousin had been hesitant talking to me about her American plans. I wished she and I had had a chance to speak first because now that Aunt Inneke and Aunt Anneke knew, well, everyone would know shortly. I didn't think Ingrid wanted that, at least not until her dreams acquired substance.

"Well, I for one applaud you, my dear," Aunt Anneke, said.

"You have such a sweet and brave cousin," Aunt Inneke said, upon noticing me.

"She's Europe's Isabelle Archer," Cornelia said, joining us.

Ingrid laughed along with the others, but it sounded tense. As did her words. "If that's the case, then I'll need to act quickly if I'm to charm an elderly gentleman for his inheritance."

"With a happier outcome, I hope," my wife added.

"Who's Isabelle Archer?" I said, after the mirth died down.

"The heroine from a Henry James novel," Ingrid said.

"'Portrait of a Lady,' Wim," Cornelia said, and then to the others, "My husband doesn't read novels, finds them morally lacking." She said it matter-of-factly, as if having accepted this fault as charming long ago.

"Really, Cornelia," I said.

Aunt Inneke bristled, as she always did when encountering conflict. "When do you intend to depart, dear?"

For some reason, Ingrid glanced at Cornelia, then at me. She seemed uncomfortable again as she said, "I—I can't say at the moment . . ."

"What my cousin is trying to explain," I said, "is that her plans are still in the wishing stage."

Both Ingrid and Cornelia stared at me as if I'd said something stupid, increasing poor Aunt Inneke's discomfort. She and her sister then excused themselves, leaving me with my wife and cousin, confused. I expected one of them to explain but neither did. Relief came in the form of my father-in-law who joined us then.

"Daddy, can I share your surprise now?" Cornelia said, putting an arm through his.

"Absolutely," he said, patting her wrist. "It's all set."

"Wim, you'll love what my father's giving us for our fifth anniversary."

"I will, will I?"

"I'm sending you two abroad for a week, the first week in July," her father said, nodding eagerly.

"Daddy, I was going to tell him," Cornelia said, drowning out an odd gasp from Ingrid.

"Sorry," Mr. van Rozebout said.

"That sounds nice," I said, "but how can I go away for that long when I've been refusing shorter vacation requests from my staff?"

"I'm ahead of you there, son." He paused, no doubt realizing, as I did, that he had never referred to me with such intimacy before. "Anyway," he continued, "I've decided it's high time we let Jaap Vos take a hand at the reins, to test him out, to watch him in action."

"I see," I said, trying to keep calm. My instincts told me my father-in-law was looking to make this a permanent change.

"Isn't that great?" Cornelia said.

"Forgive me for saying so, but I'm not sure Jaap's up to such responsibility yet."

"He'll have to be," Cornelia's father said. Then he burst out laughing as he figured out the nature of my thoughts. He put his hand on my shoulder and began to shake his head profusely. "Oh my, I'm sorry. I didn't mean to alarm you, Wim. You see, my health is beginning to wane, and my dear wife wants me at home more."

"Get to the point, daddy," Cornelia said.

"Yes, yes. Anyway, my intention is to have you take over the business sooner rather than later. We need fresh, young blood in charge, someone who's better in tune with the times, business wise, someone who can carve our path into this century and beyond. You more than proved yourself as that man in Marseille."

"Isn't that wonderful?" Cornelia said, with extreme pride and no attempt to hide her prior knowledge of this.

It was wonderful and I was dumbstruck. Since its inception, no one but a full-blooded van Rozebout had ever been in charge of the shipping company. This change had to have been approved by my father-in-law's brothers. That explained my popularity at the party, not Ingrid.

"I'd be honoured," I said, smiling.

"That's better," Mr. van Rozebout said, and we shook hands.

"Where are you two going to go on your trip?" Ingrid said, her voice shaking slightly. She looked pale.

"Paris," Cornelia said, gasping the word dramatically. My wife's eyes darted between Ingrid and me, as if searching for a reaction from one of us, or both.

I gave her one. My hand jerked, half a glass of champagne spilled onto the ground. This conversation, in spite of its good news, seemed orchestrated. Ingrid's poise had disappeared too, as if she was also a victim. Cornelia stepped away from me to embrace her father and I removed my fez to cool my head.

"Paris, that is terrific," Ingrid said, her voice barely perceptible above my wife's jubilance.

Paris would not have been my choice, considering my first experience of the City of Light. And despite my ambition, the proposal to leave Jaap in charge during my absence troubled me. We had such a busy period ahead of us I didn't think he'd be up to it. I would have double the work welcoming me back just to repair his mistakes.

However, this wasn't the appropriate time to share these concerns and I decided to discuss them with my father-in-law later. And with these approving and smiling faces around me, I had to reconsider my opinion of Paris. Had I really given it a chance? Was it right to judge it solely on a single, disturbing evening? All the reasons that drew me there in the first place—the architecture, the lights, the Louvre, and of course the Eiffel Tower—nothing had changed about them.

"Yes, Paris would be wonderful," I said.

Magic words, apparently, as they induced a kiss from Cornelia, along with a warm embrace. It was rare for us to display such affection toward each other, let alone with others around.

Then a slap on my shoulder made me turn around. I nearly fainted when I saw Adam Zelle, Maggie's father, standing behind me, putting on the tallest top hat I'd ever seen.

"Are you all right, Wim?" Ingrid said.

"Did I frighten you?" Zelle said, but it was Max van Rozebout's voice. With the top hat on, Adam Zelle transformed into Abraham Lincoln, as portrayed by my brother-in-law.

"Yes, I mean no. I'm fine."

My father-in-law stepped in to introduce my cousin to Max.

"I'm a big admirer of Mr. Lincoln, such a tragic death," Ingrid said.

"Ah yes, the mortal peril of theatre boxes," Max said.

"You're late, but you do look splendid," Cornelia said.

"Thank you, but I think Wim looks the smartest of us all in that Zouave get-up. Isn't it appropriate then that I happened to choose a character from America's Civil War as well?"

"Indeed . . . appropriate?" I said. "How so?"

"So that together we can emancipate this celebration from French domination. Speaking of France, my dear sister, did I hear you right, that you will be off to my adopted home soon? To celebrate my brother-in-law's deserved ascent in the family business?"

"You did and I cannot wait to see this famous dancer, Mata Hari."

Cornelia said this somewhat hesitantly, sneaking a sidelong glance at me.

"And you must see her, Cornelia, darling," said a high-pitched male voice, with a French accent. "You won't be disappointed. Mata Hari virtually runs Paris these days."

It had been at least a year since I'd last seen Eric LaPlante but he still looked comical to me with his short height and slick, over-pomaded black hair. He had on a wildly yellow shirt and silver tie underneath a ruffled lime-green jacket, a casualty of a night of debauchery, no doubt.

"Voila!" Max said, more to his sister than to anyone else, as if Eric's presence was his gift.

Rather than embracing Eric with the warmth that often incited a bout of jealousy within me, Cornelia greeted Max's friend and my nemesis with a frown.

"Sorry to be late," Eric said, slurring his words but still maintaining his precise but thin and high-pitched, French-accented Dutch.

"Have you been drinking?" Cornelia said.

"A drop or two, along the way," Eric said.

"We did rush," Max said, apologetically. "Nothing could make us miss my sweet sister's birthday, even if it meant abandoning the car in town and taking horses."

"You were supposed to wear a costume," my wife said to Eric, her arms crossed. "Or did you have to abandon that too?"

It was hard to tell whether this was Cornelia's usual light-hearted bantering or whether she was truly angry. Eric just smiled, pointed at me.

"Really, Cornelia, would you have me wear something like that ghastly thing."

The rudeness of the remark barely affected me, considering the source, but caught others off guard. Ingrid, for one, but surprisingly Cornelia too, and she seemed to take the insult personally.

"I'll have you know my husband's father fought in the American Civil War to help free slaves wearing that."

"Which only goes to show what he is," Eric said, matching her cadence.

"A fighter, a man," Cornelia said. "The son of a hero."

"No," Eric said, inserting an intentional pause. "A bloodthirsty American."

Then he let out a silly laugh, a feeble attempt to convince us he had been jesting all along. Alas, my wife fell for it as always. She embraced him and found someone to get him a glass of champagne. Then she brought Ingrid forward.

"This is the Eric I told you about, the one who painted my portrait," she said, as they shook hands.

"It's a beautiful painting," Ingrid said.

"My first one, my last one," Eric said, with melodramatic flair.

"Such a waste of talent," Cornelia said. "Eric, don't you think Ingrid would make a good subject for a portrait?"

Eric stepped closer to my cousin and looked at her studiously, pretentiously, as an artist might. He nodded slowly, and Ingrid blushed under the attention.

"Tempting, yes. But do you mean paint her as the peasant girl she's dressed up as, or as the peasant girl she is?"

All of us, including Cornelia's father, took his crass remark in stride. Except Ingrid. There was a seething anger in her eyes I had not seen before. My cousin appeared ready for a physical altercation. My first inclination was to escort her away, but I held back, curious to see how she would handle herself.

"So what do you do then?" Ingrid said, stiffly, clearly annoyed by what he'd said, but perhaps also at me for not having intervened. "If you're unable to paint."

"I am able to paint. I just choose not to."

"Then what do you choose to do?"

"Eric's a journalist, an art critic," said Max, prompting a reproachful glare from his friend.

"An art critic, yes," Eric said, "and someone you need to be nice to, Cornelia, if you wish to see Mata Hari. Her shows are always sold out."

"Who, or what, is Mata Hari?" Ingrid said.

"I cannot believe there is a single person in Europe who has not heard of Mata Hari," Max said, chortling.

"It takes a while for news to travel to the peasant provinces," Ingrid said.

"Ah, yes, of course," Eric said, with an appreciative smile, "you must be Wim's cousin from Leeuwarden. Well then, you ought to know Mata Hari best of all."

"How could I—I don't even know who she is," Ingrid said.

"She's a stage dancer in Paris, notorious for taking off her clothes," I said, trying to sound as bland as possible, hoping that would steer the discussion elsewhere.

"In public? That's obscene," Ingrid said.

"Not as far as the public is concerned," Max said. "She's the biggest sensation in Europe right now."

"That's right," Eric said. "Let me show you."

He produced a newspaper article from his jacket pocket, which he unfolded in front of her. Max lighted a long match so we could read it. I recognized the piece from the *New Rotterdam Daily* of that past Wednesday, another work disruptor I had had to confiscate from my staff. It had disturbed me as it was the first time I had seen Mata Hari explicitly confirm her Dutch heritage, as well as her marriage to MacLeod. While Ingrid scanned the article, Eric spoke.

"I've written several reviews of her shows, but this story has inspired me to do something more ambitious, a feature. And you, my dear Frisian girl," and he paused until she looked up at him, "along with your cousin, can help me."

"I'm not sure whether to be shocked or offended at such a suggestion," Ingrid said, looking away. "Or your rude arrogance."

"My, my, she is quite comely when angered," Eric said. "I might paint her after all."

"That's enough LaPlante," I said.

"All right, but let's get back to the subject at hand. Now, if the young lady can't help me out directly, I'm sure you can, Wim. After all, you were at her debut in March."

"You weren't, you didn't," Mr. van Rozebout said, half censure, half envy.

"To be fair to my brother-in-law, he didn't enjoy the dance," Max said.

"And I'm mad at you, Max, for not telling me you had taken Wim there," Cornelia said, looking more amused than angry.

"You know?"

"Wim told me all about it."

"It was a disgusting display," I said.

"People, people, you're missing the point," Eric said. "I have a feature to write and Wim and his feisty but sweet and charming cousin will be my exclusive sources for the definitive article. The one that not only solves the mystery of Mata Hari's origins, but also reveals what she's really like, now and as a young girl. Who better than you, Wim, since you grew up with her in Leeuwarden—"

"What?" Ingrid said, staring at me.

"He didn't tell you?" Eric said.

"Wait—did that have to do with those people you asked about?" Ingrid said.

"I thought the dancer was someone I knew," I said, an uncomfortable warmth rising in me.

"Precisely!" Eric was grinning now, like an overconfident prosecutor. His smugness was making me livid. "Or perhaps you hoped to reacquaint yourself with an old lover."

I grabbed him by both shoulders, lifted him up and then shoved him to the ground, shoved him hard enough to knock off his spectacles. Somehow his champagne glass remained in his hand but the contents spilled onto the lawn and several shoes.

"What the . . .," my father-in-law said, but he didn't move.

An eerie silence then. Conversations all over the estate stopped. I felt a pair of hands on my arms trying to pull me away. Whose they were I could not say because my eyes were on my adversary, but they belonged to a woman. I easily shrugged them off and stood over LaPlante's prone form, my right hand fisted, while pointing at him with my left.

"Stop him, before he . . ."

Others echoed that appeal but no one made a move. If they had, I probably would have jumped on Eric. Instead, my mind began to swirl and spin. Images passed before me: a bloodied Bart Postma; the vagrants on the d'Iena bridge near the Eiffel Tower; various other boys in Manhattan and Leeuwarden just before I beat them. However, none matched the fear and weakness I saw in Eric LaPlante's eyes. And that weakness drained my desire for violence.

I relaxed my arms, stepped back to let him get up. Several sighs of relief let out and the spectators dispersed. Eric's hands shook as he retrieved his glasses, checked them for damage, and put them on. He brushed off his trousers, his eyes avoiding mine, but appealing to Cornelia who now stood next to me.

"Now Eric, I'm only going to say this once," I said, keeping my voice low and steady. "And that goes for you too, Max. That dancer you idolize so much is not anyone I know. Yes, she reminded me of someone and, yes, I did ask around Leeuwarden about it. I did so only to ensure that was the end of it."

"Corrie, he's a madman," Eric said. "Are you going to let him—?"

"Be quiet, Eric," Cornelia said. "You asked for this. Here you come to my party, you don't even bother to respect my wishes and dress up, and then you harass my husband and his cousin, who happens to be my guest of honour tonight, just so you can research and write some stupid article."

Cornelia's reaction shocked me as much as it evidently did Eric. Nevertheless, I kept my focus on LaPlante, intent on making my point final. Not only to him, but also to those whose support and confidence I would need to run the company.

"That was the end of it because I was wrong," I continued. "Wrong, and never so happy to be wrong. The idea I would have befriended a woman capable of such a lewd public exhibition is outrageous, unconscionable, slanderous. Believe me, all coincidences aside, the dancer you saw, the dancer you admire is not anyone I have ever known, whether she is from Leeuwarden or from Java or from Paris, Moscow, or wherever. Are we clear on this?"

Eric surrendered a begrudging nod before Max ushered him toward the house. Cornelia stood close to me, a dreamy vapidity in her eyes. Then her slim body began to sway trance-like; it seemed any slight breeze would knock her over. I put my arm around her to hold her up. She grabbed my hand tight, let out a ghostly sigh, and then began quivering. I thought she would faint and clutched her close. This helped her regain her composure and she again became her elegant, stately self, albeit somewhat shaken. She walked off with her father, leaving me alone with a bewildered Ingrid.

"Wim, I don't understand what that was all about," my cousin said.

"Neither do I," I said, absentmindedly.

"No, I mean about this Mata Hari," Ingrid said. Then she handed me the article. "I thought you came to see us in Leeuwarden because of my father."

I motioned for her to walk with me around the pond to the other side. A pair of ducks were gliding in the water—mother and duckling—as they paralleled our route. Frogs jumped from one lily pad to another, raising splashes. We sat at a small bench from where we could see the main house. A waiter provided us fresh champagne. Ingrid took a glass but set it down. I took a large sip from mine. Then another, before I told her about the events in Paris, about how I feared Margaretha Zelle, the one I had asked Ingrid about in March, had fallen into disgrace. However, as I had done with my wife, and intended to do with everyone from then on, I left out the interviews with Mrs. Huizenga and Mr. Zelle, saying only the family had moved away, leaving no evidence Margaretha—I had to be careful not to say Maggie—ever had been in Paris.

It was a gamble, I knew, but I hoped by the time the truth came out, if it ever did, no one would care. If necessary, I could act shocked and claim I was wrong about being wrong. But it seemed as if Ingrid believed every word.

The bigger issue for me was how my lying was becoming a habit, with no sense of the motivation behind it. Why was it so important for me to keep this hidden? Especially as it seemed to do nothing but isolate me from everyone. I couldn't say; neither could I shake off the feeling I had to continue doing so.

"Thank you for being honest with me," Ingrid said, and I nodded, cringing with guilt inside. "This isn't something my mother needs to know about. Really, we should only be glad and thank God we were able to come together when we did."

"I'm happy to hear you say that," I said, smiling with pleasure and relief. But then I paused. "What do you mean, when we did?"

"I can understand your distress," she said, apparently not hearing me.

"Thank you, if it wasn't for that trouble maker, Max—"

"Oh, I think you've misjudged your brother-in-law. From what I've observed, I think he admires you a great deal. I'm only relying on my first impression but I sensed he genuinely regrets doing anything to offend you."

"Then why would he embarrass me by bringing up the Leeuwarden business?"

"I think his peculiar little pal might have had more to do with it than you think."

"You don't like Eric?" I said.

I shook my head.

"He's the type of man I'll be glad to leave behind when I go to America."

I chuckled, glad to have an ally on that subject. Still, her mention of America saddened me, particularly the assured tone in her voice.

A collective hush from the house made us look up. Cornelia was standing alone on the little balcony that overlooked the lawn. She was watching us, her arms crossed while she sipped from her champagne flute, but too far away for me to read her expression. Then her father joined her, followed by Mrs. van Rozebout holding a sleepy Antje against her shoulder. I was unsure if I should join them. When I waved, no one responded. Then Cornelia turned her head to face the starry, black sky and the big moon, toward which the others now turned.

"Look out there," I said, to Ingrid, who had also been looking at the balcony.

She did so just in time to watch the first of many green, red, white, and purple showers of sparks exploding and falling from high above. Some paled in the glow of the nearly full moon resting much higher in the heavens. Twenty-five tiny rockets in all, one for each year. Every fifth one, we raised our glasses, as did the other guests, in salute to my wife, which clearly delighted Cornelia.

"In America," I said, "we light small candles on a cake—say, there's a Yankee tidbit for you."

"I read something about that somewhere," she said, but her smile seemed forced and sad.

"Well, we'll do something like that for Antje, for her second birthday in December. You and your mother will come. I'll send a car."

"Oh, I don't know. That's so far off. And the weather."

"Nonsense, Ingrid. It's important for Antje, and for me, that you take an active part in her life."

My words came out in a funny way. Ingrid smiled but didn't say anything. We continued watching the brilliant colours and listening to the shoots and crackles of the gunpowder. Then Ingrid put her empty glass on the ground.

"Wim, do you remember my comment yesterday, when I said how you and your wife are so different? At the time it was meant to be slightly critical."

"I've—I mean we've—heard such comments before."

"Maybe so, but it wasn't my place."

"Forget about it."

"That's not what I want to say. I want to apologize for any disrespect, true, but also to confess to you how wrong I was. When I saw how Cornelia looked at you, when you were talking about that horrid dancer, I saw how deeply she loves you, much more than she may have even realized till then."

The fireworks stopped and now the world became eerily quiet, smoke wafting in odd patterns through the windless sky.

"It is a beautiful night," I said.

"It must have been hard for you."

"What do you mean?" I said, looking at her, but her gaze was skyward.

"One would think wealth was something to strive for and that, given the opportunity, only a fool would decline."

"What are you talking about?" I said.

"I'm talking about you, Wim. How you came into this world of wealth. Never have I seen such a glaring example of a fish out of water."

"At your age I'm not sure you should make such conclusions, especially without knowing what I've experienced."

"I suppose you're right. I'm just imagining how it would be for me."

"Tell me then, Ingrid, if you had a chance to live like the van Rozebouts, in a place like this, would you still choose to go to America?"

"Oh yes," she said, without hesitation.

I waited for an explanation and became disappointed by her unwillingness to elaborate.

"The sooner the better, is that it?" I said. "Is your patience running out?"

She stared at me for a lengthy moment, then nodded, before offering a wan smile.

"I wasn't supposed to tell you this, at least not yet, but when you and Cornelia are in Paris next month, I will be on a ship to America."

Another spray of sparks shot up as a series of loud bangs harmonized violently with the brightening sky. Flashes of light conspired with the tall trees to cast shadows far beyond the pond. The vision reminded me of a Fourth of July celebration at Battery Park in Manhattan, when I was six or seven. I had felt lost among the crowd of shouting, exhilarated people, and lonely for some reason.

Only then, while watching the fireworks at the van Rozebout estate, did I recall that had been a week after my mother had died.

Mata Hari

I drew back the mauve curtain on the mural sized window, opening up Paris to our room, our room to Paris. Blocks and blocks of beige buildings paralleled the Seine along wide avenues. Beyond the Champs-Élysées the brilliant gardens of the Tuileries rolled out like a magnificent rug, leading to the yellowish magnificence of the Louvre. The Ile de la Cité, the spires of Notre Dame, a sun-washed urban vista.

"What a view," I said. "Now this is the Paris I'd always hoped to see."

"It's warm in here. Open the window, let some air in."

I struggled, first to unlatch the window, then to push it open. The breeze that entered, in my opinion, actually made the room warmer. But that wasn't why Cornelia let out a groan when she poked her head out and glanced left and right.

"The Eiffel Tower, where is the Eiffel Tower?" she said, as if it were my fault. "I specifically requested a room looking out on the Eiffel Tower."

A trivial concern over a view. Was this it? I wondered. Was this what would burst the bubble of marital bliss I had enjoyed for more than a month?

So much changed after Cornelia's birthday, most notably a degree of affection from my wife I hadn't enjoyed since our early courtship days. Not just affection, but deference too, beginning the morning after the party.

The roads had dried and, to our delight, my father-in-law had sent Jacob out before dawn to retrieve the motorcar from town. Mr. van Rozebout roused me early, anxious to teach me how to drive the thing; apparently Max wasn't as careful with it as my father-in-law would have liked. Driving came naturally to me and I was an expert before breakfast. I announced I would chauffeur everyone to the beach. Then Cornelia shocked me by insisting all of us, including Max—thankfully, Eric had gone with Jacob and not stayed over—attend church first. The funny thing was I had been so engrossed with the car I'd forgotten it was Sunday.

This turnaround was no anomaly. Back in Amsterdam, Cornelia happily attended church regularly. It didn't stop there. Indeed, my wishes on most everything took priority in our house. Fewer struggles at home made it easier for me to concentrate on the tripled workload at the office. Upon my return, I had to fire two men for incompetence and hire four more right away, and then ensure they became productive quickly. Furthermore, I had to work with my eventual successor, Jaap Vos, to prepare for my upcoming absence. I tried to cover all possible scenarios. It was difficult keeping Jaap focused; my upcoming weeklong absence could prove disastrous. And then I also began to assume a number of Mr. van Rozebout's tasks and responsibilities.

Cornelia helped most of all by doing more to manage the house, by becoming stricter with the servants on keeping everything tidy—she was often too lenient in that regard before, in my opinion—by ensuring my newspapers were ready and in good condition for me after work, and by coordinating brief but concentrated time with Antje, and so forth. She was willing to sacrifice her shopping for less costly but more rewarding pursuits, such as excursions to Artis Zoo, Vondelpark, or simple walks along the canals. And she was the one who suggested we go to Paris without servants.

Our conversations at dinner grew longer, and more intimate. We discussed many subjects we never had before, particularly the many sights we intended to see in Paris, none of which included Mata Hari.

In fact, all mention of Mata Hari at home ceased after the party despite the increased attention given to the dancer in the newspapers across Europe. That, along with the general gossiping amongst my staff, made it only a matter of time before my lie was discovered. But if it was, I never heard about it. It helped that the stories of her history remained convoluted; some of the far-fetched versions were rather amusing.

Alas, another topic we avoided, whether intentionally or not, was my cousin's departure to America. In light of Cornelia's newfound devotion, I held back my resentment at not having an opportunity to go to Leeuwarden, if only to say farewell in person. I also had hoped to get a chance tell my cousin about Mark Dekker, who repeated his offers of assistance for Ingrid, including arranging lodgings and finding employment.

Just days prior to our leaving for Paris, on a miserably rainy evening, I arrived home in a foul mood after spending fourteen hours at the Beurs. My last opportunity to go to Leeuwarden had come and gone by then. Antje was already in bed. So when I found Cornelia languidly perusing the brochures and guidebooks, my frustration came to a boil.

"You know, Cornelia, I've never troubled you over helping my cousin."

"Why would you trouble me over that?"

She said the words nonchalantly with a blank look and now I felt less assured, as if idly stirring up trouble, rather than attempting to voice a valid concern. But if I didn't continue, I would only delay the inevitable argument.

"You should have talked to me before giving her any money. It would have been nice for us to get to know her first."

"Yes, I'm sure you would feel that way. But the truth is I didn't give her any money at all."

"Then who did?"

"No one gave her money. She was quite adamant—graciously so, I might add—that I not give her any money."

"Yet she could still afford to buy a ticket. Are you implying she stole the money?"

"Really, Wim, how could you of all people suggest something like that?"

"Well, what then?"

"Just calm down and I'll tell you."

"Thank you," I said.

"Of course Ingrid shared with me her plans during our shopping excursion. Her enthusiasm was infectious. So while your cousin was trying on several outfits at one shop, I sneaked away to our travel agent. I purchased her a one-way ticket—it doesn't cost as much as you'd think it would—and some luggage. Oh, that awful red thing she showed up with—"

"Cornelia, please."

"Sorry, but it was awful. Anyway, I paid for the passage and arranged a hotel for her in Rotterdam so she could go the day before. I also obtained a voucher for second-class train tickets from Leeuwarden to Rotterdam. You should have seen the look of surprise on her face—ha, just like the one you have now. Only happier. Surely, she told you all this in Brielle."

Not all of it. Until then, I had thought Ingrid had simply chosen the first ship out of Holland. "The timing is oddly coincidental," I said.

"Well . . ."

"Well, what? It sounds as if you were trying to get rid of her."

"That's a rather crass way of putting it. I was merely trying to make everyone happy."

"So I'm right. But why?"

She regarded me for some time before answering.

"Oh Wim, you innocent man, you miss so much. If only you could have seen how your cousin looked at you."

"What, are you saying it was jealousy? That's why you arranged our Paris trip for the same time as her departure? Jealousy?"

"I'm not—I don't mean to say—perhaps she herself doesn't know. It's something a woman can detect in another woman."

"Ingrid and I are cousins. Cousins don't marry. They may in your world—I'm sure one could discover plenty of examples in the van Rozebout lineage—but not in mine. How could you conceive such a contemptible thought, let alone speak it."

My wife stared at me, as if the man she married, who was not her cousin, had uttered the most imbecilic statement ever. I stared back. Our eyes remained locked until her lips turned up in a curious smile.

"You can't keep her pure and innocent forever," she said.

"What on earth does that mean?" I said, for some reason thinking she was referring to Antje.

Cornelia started walking away. I grabbed her arm. Her head jerked as she shook her arm out of my hand and left the room.

I learned long ago that on such occasions it was best not to go after her, to give my wife, as well as me, a moment to calm down. I used my moment to analyze, as objectively as I could, what had transpired. Something about this exchange was different from those in the past. Cornelia's vulnerability. This time my wife lacked a wilfulness to win the battle, which told me this meant something to her, that she was not arguing for the sake of the conflict, but for something more. Cornelia returned several minutes later, contrite. With the accumulated goodwill of the previous weeks, this touched me and I felt bad for my part in the argument.

Fortunately, that incident passed and nothing occurred again until this outburst over the Eiffel Tower-less view, just at the time when my cousin might have arrived in Rotterdam, excited, frightened, but alone, left to wait out the hours until she would board the ship.

"Go to the concierge and complain," Cornelia commanded. "Please," she added, her smile gracious, her eyes twinkling.

I left, not so much to grant her wish, but to get out before saying something I'd regret. I walked down the long red-carpeted hallway, taking the stairs instead of the lift, giving me more time to compose myself. I had to wait until the clerk finished checking in a couple from Lyon before I could explain my wife's concern. His smile was genuine, his manner courteous and responsive, and he seemed to appreciate the quality of my French.

"*Monsieur*, we do apologize with utmost sincerity," he said. "Unfortunately, many of our guestrooms are under repair and the others are being used by long term guests. But, *Monsieur Brink*, you must have noticed your suite is larger—"

"Larger? Larger than what?"

"—and very finely appointed with the most modern furnishings and decor, and on a high floor. It is, in all other respects, superior to the one you reserved."

Since Cornelia or her father had arranged the accommodations, I couldn't argue that point. "My wife had her heart set on seeing the Eiffel Tower from out our window," I said.

"It is unfortunate but the situation is out of my control," he said, shrugging. "The view you enjoy now, you must concede, is magnificent. In the distance you can even see Montmartre where they are building the Sacré-Coeur Cathedral. Maupassant would approve."

"Who is Maupassant?"

"You do not know of our famous writer, Guy de Maupassant?" he said, with a hurt look.

"A writer, you say. I suppose my wife might have heard of him. Why would this writer approve, and my wife not?"

"M. de Maupassant is not a lover of our city's now most famous structure. So he eats at the restaurant there whenever he can. Why? Because it is the only place in Paris where he can eat out without seeing the Eiffel Tower."

He let out a sharp laugh and, despite my mood, I couldn't resist a smile. The clerk then reached into a cubbyhole behind him.

"Oh, M. Brink, I almost forgot, I have here a message for you and your wife."

I slid the small envelope inside my jacket pocket, more concerned about how to report my lack of success to Cornelia, part of me wishing for the buffer of servants.

The sun from the window blinded me briefly when I opened the door. The same gentle warm breeze came from the opened window. I became worried until I heard the splashing water telling me she was attending to her toilet. I began to unpack our suitcases. It had been a long and wearisome train ride but I had plenty of energy for a casual walk in the neighbourhood.

"Cornelia?"

"Yes?"

"I couldn't do anything about the view, but why don't we go for a walk and see the Eiffel Tower up close? It's just across the river."

"I see," she said, almost as if she'd forgotten why I'd left. "Don't go anywhere. I'll be out in a moment."

I stood by the window and felt disorientated at the view of the city. The sky was so clear, the mid-afternoon sun high above and shining on Paris's left bank. In the distance stood the hill of Montmartre, where I could spot the scaffolding of the large cathedral under construction, the dark shapes of tiny workers moving about, just as the clerk had described.

A sharp tingle went through my body as my wife's delicate hands grasped at the neck of my jacket and then pulled at my shoulders. Her touch was light and angelic, and then I felt her bosom as it brushed against my back. A sweet odour, like a gentle perfume tinged with vanilla, filled the air.

"You know, Wim, this is a splendid view."

"Of course it is. From here, we can see much more of Paris . . ."

"Wim."

"Yes, Cornelia."

"Please count to three, slowly, in French, and then turn around."

She released her hold. As I counted, a cloud diffused the sunlight, exposing a few specks of dust on the windowsill. The cloud passed quickly, forcing me to squint as I turned around.

There stood Cornelia, my wife, in the middle of the room, slim and vulnerable in a translucent mint green gown. Its sheerness was such that the light from the window shone through to reveal the paleness of her skin, the curves of her slender form, and more. Behind her, a whitish candle, the source of the vanilla aroma. A white silk belt wrapped the gown tight to her body. Her eyes held a feral brightness.

"What is it?" I said.

She put a finger to her mouth and then began to sway her body back and forth, somewhat self-consciously at first. She paused once to compose herself, then smiled strangely before starting anew. She put out her hands and, fingers splayed, began to weave back and forth, like a cobra in an eastern bazaar. She held her small hands out for a long moment before sliding them to her hips. She stopped to unclasp the silk belt, dropping it to the floor, then slowly removing the gown until a pile of pale green cloth crumpled on the rug. My eyes stared down a long moment before I noticed she had begun her movements again. I coughed and my face turned red.

"What's the matter?" Cornelia said, with an affected voice, husky and breathy.

My breath constricted, keeping me mute. Looking slightly alarmed, Cornelia approached me but when she touched me, I recoiled. She touched me again. But all I could think of was how to keep her away from the open window at which I imagined a crowd watching from the buildings across the street. In my failed, clumsy effort, I shoved her away, harder than intended. Hard enough she fell toward the bed and on it. But not hard enough that she couldn't bounce right back up to show me the contempt in her eyes. She tried to gather up her clothes but they were too flimsy and fell through her fingers. She gave up and instead pulled the bedcover and wrapped it about herself.

"Get out," she said.

"I, I . ."

"Get out!"

Then she picked up an ashtray and threw it at me, knocking me on the shoulder. As I bent to pick it up, she ran into the bathroom, locking the door behind her. After several seconds, I heard sobs, but they stopped quickly.

"Cornelia?"

Again, silence, before I heard shuffling steps on the linoleum, then water running.

"Cornelia, I demand you come out now."

The creak of the door as it opened caught me by surprise. There my wife stood, without any clothes on, in full sight of the window. She was stunningly beautiful, yet the sight repelled me. I turned away.

"That's right, husband of mine, turn your back to me, your wife. I understand it now. You think of me as sinful, don't you, just like that dancer of yours. Prude. No, don't say a word. Oh, what kind of life can we women have who are not as pure as your precious cousin?"

~~~~~~~~

An hour of wayfaring through Parisian streets concluded at the Tuileries in one of the public chairs by a fountain. I was surrounded by grassy gardens brightened by brilliant orange, red, and white flowers. The sun from behind me shone on the Place de la Concorde, where the shimmering gold leaf atop the obelisk pierced the sky. Tourists and residents, some with small dogs on thin leather leashes, a few with parasols to ward off the sun, were out enjoying idle strolls. Others relaxed in chairs, reading novels and guidebooks, newspapers and magazines, or simply talking to friends. Many smoked: cigarettes, cigarillos, cigars. Occasionally a flock of pigeons would congregate toward someone distributing stale bread. A glorious day in an idyllic spot, exactly the kind of peaceful Parisian pleasure I'd determined not to miss this time.

Then about fifteen art students stormed in and occupied the last few chairs, leaving some forced to stand or sit on the ground. Most began sketching statues and flowers with charcoal sticks, while several, with no instructor in sight, chatted. One of the more attractive young ladies reminded me of Cornelia, as she might have been as an eighteen-year-old posing for another student.

What had come over her? Never in the past had Cornelia acted in such a manner as an hour ago in the hotel room; her modesty in private was a trait I had always cherished. Our marital relations had always been discrete and purposeful. And as far as I knew, the subject of another child had not been hinted at recently, let alone discussed. Even if it had, how could she think such an ill-advised seduction, such an uninhibited display, would ever appeal to me? In daylight at that, with the curtains wide open. Was she mocking me in some way?

Ingrid's remarks about how deeply Cornelia loved me came back to me then. Perhaps I hadn't taken my cousin seriously enough. This trip was the first occasion for my wife and I to share a bed since before Antje's birth; maybe Cornelia's intent had been simply to please me. In fact, that seemed obvious now. I cringed to think how my rejection must have hurt such a proud, beautiful woman.

The damage was done, though, and I needed to give her time to calm down; I couldn't just rush back to apologize, to explain, even if a suitable explanation that wouldn't worsen matters came to me. Yet I couldn't stay at the Tuileries all day either. A cruise on the Seine in a *bateaux mouche* sounded inviting, except we had planned to do that together. The same with the Louvre.

Someone vacated the chair next to mine, abandoning a newspaper. I reached for it, shook out some crumbs, and skimmed through until I stopped at yet another article on Mata Hari, an interview. A sigh of relief upon seeing the by-line wasn't Eric's. The article included a photograph of the dancer, resplendent in her gowns and jewels, arms spread out, and her lovely head held high with that haughty expression still impressed on my mind. Unlike other photographs I'd heard about, this one was tasteful. A caption beneath the picture announced Mata Hari would be dancing tonight at Trocadéro.

Echoes of the nausea I felt four months earlier at the Guimet came over me. Was there nothing else of interest in Paris? Why was everyone so obsessed with this woman? It seemed her fame would never diminish, that I would be forever living with my lies, that I could never escape knowing this was Maggie and that any young girl in this age would be susceptible to such a fate. I reached in my pocket for the note from the clerk, knowing whom it would be from, and what it would say.

"Meet me tonight, after dinner, at the Trocadéro Palace, across the Seine from the Eiffel Tower. You can't miss it. I have a special anniversary surprise for you."

"Aha," I said, loudly, drawing hostile looks from several students. One boy glared at me as if I had permanently crippled his concentration. His sketch of a pair of trees by the rue de Rivoli entrance gate showed talent. The dullness of the subject, however, disappointed me.

I could have crumpled up Max's invitation and tossed it away, claiming I'd lost it, but who knew what problems that would create? Better to present the note to Cornelia in the spirit sent; indeed, doing so might help repair the damage I had done.

It was quiet and dark in the room, all the curtains pulled shut, making it impossible to guess it was only late afternoon. The breeze coming through the window was cooler now, pleasant. I found my wife in bed, under the covers, wearing the now wrinkled dress she had worn on the train, her hat on a table beside her, shoes on the floor. Her eyes were wide open, no longer full of the intense wildness of an hour before, but still filled with revulsion, and sadness.

"I suppose this is how you would prefer to see me?" she said.

We stared at each other for some time, more with curiosity than emotion, before I handed her the note. "It's from Max," I said. She grabbed it from me, sat up, and read it quickly. After a quick glance my way, she pushed aside the covers and stood up. "What kind of surprise do you think he has in mind?" I asked, feigning ignorance.

She shrugged. "I guess I'll find out."

"Do you want me to come, or not?" I said.

"That's up to you," she said, indifferently.

"Then I'll come," I said.

"Suit yourself. I'm hungry."

I took the hint and left to reserve a table at the hotel restaurant. Meanwhile Cornelia went to change into finer clothes. She was humming a popular song in front of the mirror when I returned, but stopped when she noticed me. Other than polite small talk and instructions to our waiter, the meal remained quiet. I'd never been so anxious to see my brother-in-law.

She didn't even look up or show any interest when we crossed under the Eiffel Tower during our silent walk to Trocadéro, a coliseum-like building of Moorish architecture, flanked by two tall towers. Long lines of people fanned out from the entrance, with more arriving every minute; on foot, by carriage, and by motorcars drawing equal amounts of disgruntlement and admiration. An atmosphere of anticipation similar to the Guimet, but on a larger scale.

My brother-in-law found us first. He looked dashing in his grey waistcoat, tails, and pointed leather shoes. His waxed moustache had grown too and stood up almost vertically, like radio antennae or rather, amusingly, like the Trocadéro's two towers. In this humid evening air, I suspected his grooming efforts would not hold up for long. Max reached into a breast pocket in his coat, pulled out two tickets for tonight's show, and handed them to his sister.

"Your anniversary gift," he said, before lighting a cigarette.

They were not general tickets, but for a box in the balcony. When Cornelia realized this, she beamed at her brother and cast a sidelong glance at me. It hurt me because it told me she'd only been humouring me all this time; her desire to see Mata Hari dance hadn't waned one bit since her birthday party. Her reaction exposed the tension between us but Max acted as if nothing was amiss.

"Who will join us in the box?" I said, to Max.

"Ah Wim, you can speak, after all. How is your delightful cousin?"

"Packing for America?" Cornelia said.

"Too bad, she might have appreciated this."

What motivated my brother-in-law to say something so callous and uncalled for was beyond my comprehension, but I let it go. How naive Ingrid had been in believing Max admired me. Clearly, she did not understand such men.

"Just tell me who is to join us in the box," I said, bracing myself for a certain name.

"No one. It is a box for four, but, as it is your anniversary, the other two seats will remain empty so you can be alone with each other."

Cornelia let out a smirk. I moved to take the tickets from her but she resisted, possibly worried I'd tear them up. Truly, I was beyond such pettiness. But I didn't press her.

"Why are you dressed this way?" I said.

"I have another engagement," he said, but did not explain what it was.

"By yourself?" Cornelia said.

I didn't see his response because my eyes were drawn to several cracks in the cobblestone in which were lodged a pair of cigarette butts. For some reason, I wanted to pick them up if only to remove them from my sight. The sharp yelp of a tiny dog from behind startled me. I looked around but couldn't locate the little beast. When I turned back to Cornelia and her brother again, they were regarding me with curious looks.

"Go with your brother," I said, a split second before I realized what I was saying. But once I did, I knew it was the right thing to say. "Just the two of you," I said, in answer to their baffled expressions.

"But why?" Cornelia said, after several seconds passed.

"I have no interest in seeing this but Max does, and you obviously do as well. Who am I to get in your way and spoil your enjoyment?"

"Do you mean it?" Max said.

"Of course I mean it."

His bewilderment bewildered me. I believed that in giving us this gift, he actually thought I'd want to go, as if I shared this obsession like any common man. Despite what had happened at the Guimet.

"What will you do in the meantime, Wim?" Cornelia said.

"How long is the performance?"

"There are acts beforehand," Max said, still sounding unsure about going in my place, but less so. "Two hours, maybe three."

I shrugged, as if two hours was two minutes, and then pointed at the Eiffel Tower. "Maybe I'll climb to the top of that ugly structure, both sides, several times."

"Oh, I forgot about Eric," Max said.

"Eric?" Cornelia and I said, in unison.

"Yes, he was the one who arranged the box for you. He still feels awful for what happened at your party."

"He should," Cornelia said, cautiously, "but where is he?"

"Waiting for me at a bistro on the Champs-Élysées, near the Arc. He didn't think he'd be welcome here."

"I see," my wife said. "Wim, since you're not joining us, why don't you find Eric and tell him about the change in plans?"

I stifled a groan at what seemed a harsh penalty for my tolerance, my sacrifice. On the other hand, it was a light one considering my behaviour in the hotel room. I nodded.

"Good, and why don't you then ask him—never mind, just say hello from me, will you? And thank him."

"You don't want to see him?" I said.

"Actually, Cornelia," Max said, "I had hoped you and Wim would meet up with us at the bistro afterward."

"Of course I can go there," she said. "Will you come too?" she added, addressing me. By her tone it was unclear whether she wanted me there or not.

"If not, I'll be at the hotel," I said.

My wife then gave me a lukewarm embrace. Whether in the spirit of the moment, or laying a seed for future peace, I sincerely wished them an enjoyable evening.

Once they blended into the ever-growing throng, I regretted promising to find Eric. I was tempted to ignore the request, to leave him waiting. Not out of spite but to avoid seeing the dandy. As I'm sure he would have wanted to avoid me. But I had made a promise.

The instant I reached avenue Kleber, all this heaviness departed. My spirit turned unusually light, lazy, easy. Even the distastefulness of an encounter with Eric lost its intensity; in fact, after several blocks, it seemed I had to see him.

That was when I got the first inkling of what I was about to do. But it was only a notion. If I had grasped the full nature of it then, I would never have taken the first step.

The air, windless now, was still warm, but less humid. I slowed down, my attention drawn to an isolated tree that looked lost and lonely in the urban setting. Heavy, quick clopping broke the silence and I stepped on the curb to let a four-horse carriage pass. But then it stopped too. Its window opened and a woman's head emerged from the opening, largely covered by a magnificent flowery hat. I looked away to avoid appearing rude.

"Sir," the woman said, in French, but a voice that sounded so familiar. "Trocadéro is a good twenty-minute walk the other way. I wouldn't want you to be late."

"Excuse me?" I said.

"You are most certainly on your way to watch the supreme and famous Indian dancer, the great Mata Hari, are you not?"

I approached the carriage for a closer look at the face of a person I once knew well but, as it turned out, never understood. That we would meet again, at this pivotal moment for me, had a poetic inevitability about it.

"Yes, I am who you think I am," she said.

"Yes you are, Maggie," I said, in Dutch.

"Wim Brink?" she said, shocked but clearly pleased to recognize me. "Please join me."

She shifted to make room. Her attire was colourful, fashionable, and expensive, but also surprisingly conservative. I climbed in and now mere inches separated our bodies. I drifted back to my teen years, once again a lower-middle class boy standing by a lonely tree outside Grote Kerk, or adventuring through its surrounding streets, thrilled at sharing close company with such a lovely and lively girl.

Then I noticed the man sitting opposite me. A French colonel, fat, but with an affable countenance, a man old enough to be her father. An instinctive, nostalgic pang of jealousy came over me. The colonel, on the other hand, seemed untroubled by my presence.

"Paul, please meet an old friend of mine, from my childhood, Wim Brink. Wim, this is my close and dear friend, Colonel Fillon."

"Ah, and from what version of Mata Hari's past would you come from?" he said, chuckling.

"The truest one," I said.

They smiled at me as one would at a child saying something cleverly adult. Yet I didn't feel patronized. Not at all. I felt an affinity toward the officer who, in some ways, reminded me of my father, and in other ways, Opa Geert. He offered his open hand and I took it, matching his hard grip. Then Maggie shifted closer to me, our bodies making the slightest contact, and put her hands on my shoulders, squeezed them.

"You've gotten so tall and so strong, Wim. He would look wonderful in a uniform, wouldn't you say, Paul?"

"Indeed," the officer said, sincerely, showing no envy over the attention she was giving me. "Have you served?"

Maggie explained that, since I was American born, Dutch military service wasn't mandatory for me. The colonel stared at me, as if unsure whether to label me lucky or a coward. "He is a fighter and a protector, Paul," Maggie said, as if reading his reaction the same way. "Tell me, Wim, did you ever apologize to Bart Postma?"

"Of course," I said, although not sure whether I had or not.

"But your father served in America, right? Tell Paul about that curious uniform he wore."

I did so and the colonel listened closely, his interest genuine. He even said he had heard of my father's unit. He frowned briefly when I told him about the warm reception it had received at a costume party, but nodded approvingly when I mentioned Opa Geert's hopes for me to attend École Militaire.

"You know, son, you can always enlist. Age is not an issue. The French Army is always in search of good officers. Or you could follow your father's path and join our Zouaves in Africa."

"I have a wife, a daughter, and a successful career in Amsterdam already," I said, although the words sounded false and empty, sitting in this particular carriage.

"Civilian careers can wait," he said. "Every man ought to perform his duty for his country at some point in his life, especially someone like you who strikes me as one for order."

I smiled politely before I realized he was serious. He reached into a breast pocket, behind his impressive array of medals, and pulled out a small card. Then he found a pen, scribbled something on the front and handed it to me.

"If you are ever interested, call on me. Present this card and you will have no trouble getting through directly."

The colonel had a powerfully persuasive manner about him, which I couldn't help but respect. I imagined he'd recruited hundreds of reluctant men and probably would have made Max van Rozebout think twice too. Regardless of what Maggie was doing in her life, at least she was keeping company with upstanding people.

"You have a daughter, you were saying?" Maggie said, rather wistfully.

"Antje."

"That was my mother's name."

I then showed her a picture of Antje. Maggie stared at it until she began to sob. Then she handed it back and told me about Nonnie, her daughter, whom she could no longer see because her husband wouldn't let her. I had heard this from her father months before but didn't let on. Her sorrow was exactly as Mr. Zelle had described, only seeing it now made it more vivid. A feeling of pity came over me. I took her warm hand in mine and patted it.

"You say you have a high position in Amsterdam, Wim. You must know important people then. Perhaps you can do an old friend a favour."

"What do you mean?" I said.

"I need someone on my side, in Amsterdam, someone who knows lawyers and bureaucrats, and perhaps even men like my ex-husband. That might give me a chance to see my little girl again, and maybe even have her come and live with me here in Paris someday."

This was awkward. The van Rozebout name held sway in the city and I was certain I could have done something. But the idea of aiding such a reunion troubled me and I resented Maggie for asking. In my opinion, Mata Hari would not be a suitable mother unless she terminated her career. There seemed no indication that would ever be considered.

"I'm afraid my influence is low," I said, ashamed at the lie, but feeling it was justified. "I wouldn't know where to begin."

Maggie sighed resignedly, as if she'd faced similar rejection in the past. My heart went out to her and I was tempted to retract my refusal but then the Trocadéro came into view. The colonel leaned forward.

"Well, Madame, the time has come for another stupendous performance."

"Wim," Maggie said. "won't you be my guest of honour?"

"Of course he will," the colonel said. "I'll look after him backstage. We'll share a drink, enjoy the performance, and talk some more of the military."

"I am not going inside that place," I said.

"Why not?" she said. Her hurt look reminded me of the day she told me her father was going away.

"I can't," I said. But my face must have given something away for she smiled wryly.

"Ah, you disapprove. I suppose I should not be surprised. You always were rather odd about such things."

"Whatever would make you . . .?" I said, my inability to finish the question drawing a bemused look from the colonel and a knowing smile from Maggie.

"Study the audience, the men with their women, and the women with their men. Then you will have your answer."

"I'm afraid I really must go," I said.

"But never mind all that. Why don't we talk a little longer right here?"

"What about your performance?"

"My audience will wait for me. You of all people would understand that."

We exchanged awkward smiles while the colonel discretely glanced the other way. She looked so lovely, as lovely as ever, and I felt a pull to stay with her. The pull was not as effective as it would have been once though.

Indeed, there was a stronger pull toward another path. A drastic path under any other circumstances, but next to Mata Hari and what she represented, it seemed rational.

"I'm sorry," I said, with a firmness that must have surprised her, for it surprised me.

"Yes, of course," she said, her voice cold, as if grasping everything.

Mata Hari leaned forward and instructed the driver to stop the carriage right there, more than fifty yards from the theatre. She took the colonel's card from my hand and added her signature and address on the blank side.

"Please call on me sometime, so we can talk at length. And give it some further thought, whether you can help me with Nonnie."

I took the card but said nothing. This was still Maggie, my childhood friend, for whom I would have done anything once. And she saw me as that same friend, and such a request was not out of line for such friends. But she was Mata Hari too, a woman of infamy, one whose spells had already affected my family and could surely affect an innocent child adversely.

I stepped off and watched as her carriage continued to the back of the Trocadéro Palace. I watched as she resumed her earnest but easy conversation with the colonel, while I feared for Maggie's future with speculative thoughts. They were soon lost in the darkness behind the large building inside which my wife and my brother-in-law would be anxiously awaiting the curtain to rise.

They can all have each other, I thought. If this was the way of their world, I wanted no part of it. And I didn't want Antje to be part of it either. We, my daughter and I, had another option, one that had been available a long time, but wouldn't be much longer.

Ironically, I now needed not only to see Eric LaPlante, but also to enlist his help.

I spotted the little journalist and martyred artist at the only occupied table on the bistro patio. He was smoking a cigarette and twisting his wrist every few seconds to check the time. His drab grey suit made him look slightly larger, older. My mind was cold and purposeful as I took the seat across from him. He seemed startled, but I couldn't be sure.

"I suppose you didn't expect to see me, eh?"

"No, but then again, maybe I did," he said, in his contrary manner, mustering a hesitant grin, as if ready to absorb my reprimands, my reproaches, my berating, my abuse.

"My wife sends her appreciation for your thoughtful gift. I, on the other hand—" I halted. Wasted words. A sarcasm-laden lecture from me would make no difference. Not to the past, the present, and certainly not to the future. "I, on the other hand," I started again, "have declined and asked Max to accompany my wife in my place."

"I see," Eric said.

His lack of reaction grated on me. A waiter came and I ordered a bottle of champagne, and some caviar. My nemesis kept looking at me, dumbfounded no doubt.

"I'm curious," I said.

"About?"

"About your gall, about how, after what happened in Brielle, you would offer such—"

But then I stopped for the same reason as a moment ago. Interrogating him about arranging the box, or any sign of intimidation from me, rather than deter future behaviours, might actually encourage them. I no longer had it in me to fight the whole Mata Hari business, to fight Paris, Eric, Max, my wife and the world and their fascination with the dancer.

"Actually," I said. "I am curious as to why you never pestered my cousin after the party for information for your article."

"You meant to ask why I offered Cornelia, and you, those tickets, didn't you?"

"All right," I said, with a shrug. "Why did you?"

"My editor cancelled the story," he said.

"Oh?" I said, taken aback slightly at this mundane answer to my first question, glancing at him dubiously. "Why?"

"Lack of a unique perspective. There's a glut of Mata Hari stories." He stared at me as if this was my fault. "As to the other question . . ."

He said something but I wasn't listening. I was gazing through him at the Arc de Triomphe. How odd it was that the horses, carriages, and other vehicles obediently circled the archway counter-clockwise en route to connecting to one of the twelve wide avenues radiating away, while none ventured to shortcut the circle and head straight through the opening. Of course, doing so might result in a fine from the police. Yet even the pedestrians seemed to keep to the perimeter outside the two pillars rather than penetrating the opening, as if it were a fearsome portal to another world.

The waiter came with the order and filled our glasses. Eric waited until I took a sip from mine before doing the same. Did he expect a toast? I began spreading a cracker for myself.

"What's all this for?" Eric said, watching me guardedly.

"Eric," I said, pausing to swallow the cracker, "I want you to go to the Trocadéro and join Max and Cornelia."

"You're not serious," he said, as he started to help himself.

"Completely serious. Not only that, I want you and Max to take my wife out afterward, show her the Paris she's always yearned to see. Keep her out till dawn, I don't care. Make this a Parisian night she will never forget. A night Paris will never forget."

"I—I don't understand."

"It's simple," I said, striving to keep my voice calm, businesslike, "I received a somewhat elliptical telegram from work. I believe there's trouble there I have to address in person. Only I don't want anyone to get wind of it until I get there."

"Oh?" he said, sceptically. "Really?"

"Yes, and I need to go tonight so I can be there first thing in the morning. Because I want to pick up Antje on the way. That way, when Cornelia decides to come home, she needn't bother stopping at Brielle."

He took a moment to take this in during which I refilled our glasses.

"Is that the real reason you're leaving?"

"What do you think?" I said.

"I have no idea what to think. Your mouth is speaking one thing while your eyes say another. Why do I have this feeling that by helping you out, by following your instructions, I may end up hurting my dear friend, Cornelia?"

I sighed impatiently. I had hoped it wouldn't come to this but I needed to rid myself of this doubting obstacle. I gave him Colonel Fillon's card, showed where Mata Hari had signed it, with her name followed by, "Maggie," in brackets. Eric studied the card closely, judging its authenticity probably, before lifting his head, eyes wide open with wonder and, something I'd only seen looking down on him on the lawn at Brielle: respect. Only without fear this time.

"Maggie. Then you did know . . . she is the same girl . . ."

"Go ahead and write your article, Eric. This card will get you an interview. And if you say to her what I'm going to instruct you to say, it will be your best chance to get the story you want."

"What's that? Tell me."

"Not yet. You must wait until Cornelia is back in Amsterdam before you contact Mag— Mata Hari. My wife cannot know about this until you publish your article. If she finds out earlier, I can and will sabotage your efforts."

"You can trust me," Eric said.

"Yes. Nonetheless, I'm withholding the rest of the information for a few days, just to be sure. Don't take offence at that. Part of it is to make sure you wait but it's also to give me time to phrase everything properly."

"That's not necessary."

"Otherwise she might not believe you. Check your mail daily."

"All right," he said.

That my threat was unenforceable didn't matter to me; it wasn't as if I had much choice. He became twitchy now, no doubt anxious to get away before I changed my mind. He made a move to go and I didn't stop him. I watched him set off toward the Arc de Triomphe before turning down Avenue Kleber.

As his figure disappeared, a strange energy began to flow through my body, my mind. I'd never felt so feverish and so alive at the same time before.

And never so isolated. But I would fix that shortly, God willing.

Antje

The steamer destined for New York City—a slanting wall of black iron towering ominously yet quietly along the quayside—was only one of several passenger ships lined up along the Wilhelminakade. The rising sun, having already dispersed the morning mist, now chiselled away at the clouds. A sharp odour, a mix of humanity and industry, permeated the air. Farther along the quay it became stronger in proportion to the loudness of the men with their clanging shovels and foul language. Several lights silhouetted four of them, covered in soot, shovelling coal from a barge into buckets, which were then lifted onto the ship and into its belly. Judging by the shrunken hill of coal, they had been at it all night. Their movements, strong, powerful, and filled with purpose, invigorated me.

Antje stirred then, this being her usual waking hour; this however not being her usual waking place, she began to squirm anxiously.

"Hush, my sweet child. I'm here. We're here. Miraculously, we're here."

And I truly believed it was a miracle, and that God had provided divine assistance to get us to Rotterdam. How else to explain my ability, after Eric left the bistro, to disregard all distractions and focus my attention on only two things at a time, the task I was performing and the one upcoming. A single doubt at any point could have snuffed out my momentum.

I went to the hotel only long enough to get money and pack a single suitcase of clothes. I was quick enough to catch the last train for Amsterdam, getting off at Breda. From there it took a relay of occasionally reluctant cabs through the countryside to get to Brielle and my in-laws' estate, which I reached in the middle of the night. Luckily, Jacob answered the door without waking the rest of the house. While lying to Eric had caused me no qualms, doing so to the van Rozebout's dependable and helpful manservant proved more difficult. Especially because he so readily accepted the explanation I had falsified for Eric. I waited anxiously while he retrieved my daughter; it seemed wiser to let him do it and not risk waking everyone with my heavier footsteps traipsing through the house. Still, I feared Antje crying or some other disruption. Not only that, I wasn't sure of the best route to take to Rotterdam. But when Jacob gave me Antje, he seemed to discern my dilemma, and my urgency. He suggested I take the motorcar, avoid the unreliable cabs and ferries, and cross the Maas at Spijkenisse. The roads were wonderful once we crossed the bridge and we arrived at the Rotterdam port just as dawn was breaking.

The doors of the Holland-Amerika ticket office were opening now and I was first in line. To my relief, there were plenty of first-class cabins available.

"Name, please?"

"Brink—no, Terpstra," I said.

"First name?"

"I. Just the initial, I."

"Very good," he said.

"I'll need a crib."

"That can be arranged with a steward on the ship."

And it was that simple. No questions. No strange looks or reaction to my shaking hands, my unkempt appearance, or that I was a man alone with a baby. But then why would the clerk care as long as I had the money? I called for a porter and told him to leave my suitcase at the office until I directed him to put it on the ship; I didn't want to presume anything. Then Antje and I made our way toward the large vessel, which looked so tame in daylight, leashed to the bollards.

The quay was much busier now. Swarms of passengers and senders-off, porters, crew, and dockworkers bustled about. Entrepreneurs were doing a brisk business selling kits of cutlery, blankets, basins, and drinking cans to steerage passengers. Some even offered mattresses. A search amongst this chaos would be fruitless, I thought, and it seemed better to select a spot every passenger would be likely to pass. And this I did, after purchasing a fresh loaf of bread and some milk to share with Antje while we waited.

Watching these excited emigrants longing for a new world of opportunity, unaware of the miserable six to nine days on an unpredictable ocean they'd have to endure, reminded me of when my father and I had done the same, coming from America. The thrill of the sea voyage offset the smells and bad air. I never got seasick, unlike my poor dad.

Two women passed by us, dressed alike in light beige frocks, brown shoes, and fashionable but inexpensive hats that looked stiffly new. They were walking slowly, chattering away. I let Aunt Josephine and Ingrid get ten yards ahead before approaching them. The look of delight and surprise on my aunt's face came as such a relief, and provided the approval I hadn't realized I'd desperately needed.

"How kind of you to come all this way to see Ingrid off. In my heart, I had hoped you might— oh, and what a treasure. May I?"

"Of course," I said, handing over a mildly resistant Antje.

"Watch out, Mother, she pinches."

I had forgotten about that. Antje had even pinched me the night before at Brielle before realizing it was me.

Ingrid's mother brushed aside the warning and held my daughter up in the air displaying greater strength than I would have expected. Antje loved it and began to giggle and even put her arms around my aunt's neck when she came down. No pinches.

"She adores you," I said.

"Shouldn't you be in Paris, with Cornelia?" Ingrid said, a trace of bitterness in her tone.

It was time for the story I had concocted and rehearsed on the way. That Cornelia and I had decided to take a longer trip, to America, rather than Paris, and to join Ingrid. And that, unfortunately, Cornelia couldn't come along because she had taken ill. Furthermore, that my wife had insisted Ingrid share the cabin with me so my cousin could enjoy the trip in comfort. Only what sounded reasonable hours ago seemed preposterous now. Especially as the way Ingrid had asked indicated she had discerned the motivation behind my wife's generosity.

It was all I had, though, and I would have ventured ahead if not for the look my aunt was giving me. That, combined with my daughter's head resting contentedly against her shoulder, made my deception suffer stage fright. If lying to Eric had been easy, and to Jacob difficult, it was impossible to do to Aunt Josephine. Not only that, while my aunt would welcome the idea of her daughter not travelling alone, and would be relieved Ingrid could avoid the hazards of steerage, she would not be pleased about my cousin sharing a cabin with a young man. Even a young man as trustworthy as me.

Then I got the sense—and it may have been my imagination—that they weren't pleased to see me after all. They seemed to act—I may have been imagining this too—as if my presence was an unexpected inconvenience, an unwanted intrusion. Ingrid appeared more anxious to join the throng of poor immigrants on their way to America than to spend these last moments in Europe talking with a cousin she might never see again. And here I was, seeing myself as the heroic gentleman, offering to escort my cousin safely across the thousands of miles of ocean, sacrificing everything but my daughter, while also expecting gratitude. It was all collapsing. The decision I had made in Paris now revealed itself for what it truly was, as it would have to my aunt, to my cousin, to the world: an act of criminal lunacy.

"Wim," my aunt said, "are you all right?"

"Mother, I should probably go if I want to secure one of the better berths."

"Just a moment, Ingrid," my aunt said.

Both women gazed at me, my cousin with impatience but my aunt with shrewdness and wisdom. My intentions, and everything behind them seemed nakedly exposed.

"What's going on, Wim?" she said, now glancing between Ingrid, Antje, and myself.

I was close to panic.

But I'd booked the ticket under Terpstra, not Brink. I had done so to cover my tracks, or so I thought at the time. Maybe I had had a more noble intention in mind all along; perhaps that was the true miracle propelling me here.

"I'm all right," I said, smiling more broadly than I had in a long time. "And there's no rush, Ingrid. Here, I have a surprise for you," I said, and handed her the ticket.

"But this is first-class," she said, upon inspecting it, a brief flash of disappointment crossing her face. "I'm not prepared for that."

Her reaction perturbed me, but then it struck me that, instead of giving her something, I was proposing to take something away. An adventure. She was young, impatient, and had her own life to live. And here I come along, compelling her to live it my way. My aunt, on the other hand, did not hide her delight and relief.

"My goodness, Wim," she said, embracing me. "This is so generous, such a blessing. Now I'll feel more comfortable while Ingrid's on the ocean."

"For us too," I said, smiling at my aunt. "Cornelia and I felt it wasn't right to allow you to travel in steerage."

"I suppose that's true," Ingrid said, warming to the idea, obviously heartened by her mother's relief. "But I won't know what to wear to the fancy dinners."

"I'm sure you'll be able to purchase a dress on board," I said, as I handed her all the money I had with me. "Enjoy your voyage and be sure to write as soon as you have an address. I know a man in Boston who can help you get settled and find employment."

Ingrid nodded but her attention seemed fixed on the money. I detected an element of greed in this girl I hadn't before. It felt oddly comforting to discover an imperfection in my cousin, a hint Ingrid might not have been as ideal a role model for Antje as I had initially thought.

"I can't believe this is finally happening," my cousin said, breaking a short but awkward silence and then embracing me. "Thank you."

"Yes, well," I said. "I would have taken care of all this much earlier if I'd had the chance to get to Leeuwarden."

"Everything in good time," my aunt said.

"I should go now," Ingrid said.

I took Antje then and stepped aside to let mother and daughter share their farewells. My daughter, as if grasping the sadness of this separation, began crying softly.

"Hush, we're going to see your momma soon," I said. My words seemed to soothe her.

Saying them soothed me too. Observing Aunt Josephine with Ingrid, watching the love and emotion between these two women who might never see each other again, misted my eyes. Ingrid gave me another warm embrace and then gave Antje a kiss before lining up to board the ship. Ingrid continually looked back at us, waving. Antje waved back too.

A small family was boarding ahead of my cousin. A young mother, father, and a daughter, no more than ten, who was holding a small crate. The little girl was talking to it, while also waving to the shore. I wondered what was inside the crate. A small animal. A cat probably, judging by the shape of the furry brown paws reaching out between the bars.

Finally, Ingrid was on board. My daughter wrapping her little arms around my neck eclipsed the sadness I felt. And then my aunt stepped closer to me.

"You could still go with her," she said.

"Excuse me?" I said.

Just then a horn blast announced the ship's imminent departure and I acted as if I hadn't heard her. But I had heard her. And her words told me she had guessed my intent in coming there, just as they told me she would not have stopped it.

"You could," my aunt said, between the loud blasts. "If you truly wanted to, if you truly thought it was right."

I smiled but shook my head. Everything was calm now within me, everything back in control. I wasn't even concerned about what might have been happening in Paris.

After the ship was out of sight and my aunt was out of tears, I persuaded her to accompany me back to France rather than travelling alone to Leeuwarden. I did not intend to return via Brielle and I needed someone to watch my daughter while I watched the road. She was hesitant at first but agreed when I told her that Cornelia didn't know I had come to Rotterdam, and that I could use her support to explain.

In Paris, I found my wife in our hotel room, alone. Eric must have played along because she wasn't shocked or angry at seeing me, probably assuming I had resolved the business matter quicker than expected. Her manner toward me remained equivocal until I brought out Antje. Cornelia was so thrilled to see our daughter, she barely listened to my explanations. Apparently she had dreamt of Antje having an accident in Brielle so she saw my taking her as a rescue, not anything else. I could have told her anything, but everything I did tell her was true, if not necessarily complete.

She not only understood my wish to see Ingrid one last time, but was also glad I had done so, saying she had felt bad since our argument just before the trip. She welcomed my aunt as warmly as she had initially welcomed Ingrid. Cornelia convinced her to stay with us and watch Antje while we enjoyed Paris. Aunt Josephine was happy to do so while we saw all the sites we could fit into those several days. I didn't see Max again on that trip, nor Eric.

Max revealed to me later that Mata Hari had not impressed Cornelia. And that she was so put off by the audience's reaction to the dancer—especially that of Max and Eric—that she left the performance early. Cornelia never told me that herself, though.

I shudder to think how close it came for Antje and me to be living in America. And for what? There had been far too much separation of children from parents in my family. Perhaps it took witnessing the heartbreaking moment between my aunt and cousin to break my spell of moral madness. My concerns about raising Antje in Europe were insignificant compared to the potential damage of taking her away from her mother. Whatever Cornelia's failings, they could never turn my daughter into a Mata Hari. Not as long as I took care of things. Not as long as I remained a good father and husband, one capable of resisting the negative influences and promoting the positive ones, each in good measure. The same determination that almost brought about such a separation could also keep my family together.

To say Cornelia and I are closer as husband and wife would be correct but it might be more accurate to say we've aligned our individual selves better. More so since Antje's sister,

Beatrix Louise, came into our lives two years later. She and her mother reside at the estate in Brielle where Cornelia can look after her parents as they approach their last days. Antje, however, to my delight, prefers to stay with me in Amsterdam on weekdays and attend school there. She hopes to study at the University of Leiden, as her father did.

Holland's neutrality has meant prosperity for the van Rozebout Shipping Company and for me too since I assumed full control a year later. I even coaxed my brother-in-law back to manage our sales office in Paris, which I plan to reopen soon, now that the war has left this city. Max has a knack for landing reluctant clients and I've worked on my ability to refrain from inquiring how.

My dear aunt has passed on but my cousin is living comfortably in the United States. Ingrid teaches English and does translations of Dutch academic books and articles, a skill for which she has gained some renown. She and Mark Dekker were close for some time—I was never clear on what that meant—but then they had a sudden, unexplained parting soon afterward.

Ingrid seems happy in America, though, in spite of her inevitable spinsterhood, but I can't discern much from her brief letters, nor could I from her single return to Europe. That was six years ago to attend her mother's funeral. I offered to pay her passage but she insisted on paying her own way. It was nice to see her, but awkward too. Behind her sweet, chaste nature there's a lingering coldness, a frigidity perhaps, which I failed to see at first.

As I had failed to see many things. But life is that way, I suppose; it's often not in one's power to see what one ought to see. But at least for me, things turned out well.

The same cannot be said for Mata Hari, of course. Even the oft-beleaguered Eiffel Tower will outlive that legend. That hunk of dirty metal, that inverted bridge abutment, is where I will see Antje later, along with her Uncle Max. Both are wisely sleeping still at his new house. Probably where I should be too, instead of this cold damp field outside Paris. I doubt Max even knows what's about to happen here. His interest in the dancer waned long ago.

Some spells get broken; others wear off.

My daughter is now the same age Maggie was that last time I saw her in Leeuwarden. A meaningless coincidence? Of course it is. As is the fact this is Antje's first visit to Paris at an age she can appreciate it. It's wonderful to watch as she grows and appreciates more and more.

And now, after looking back over those twelve and a half years, I can envision the day I retell all of this to Antje.

No one else, just Antje.

The Spy

At last, the curtain of fog lifts to reveal the naked dawn. The hushed, conspiratorial tittle-tattle blathering of the crowd, like that of birds scavenging for food, blends in with the sounds of the wind-tussled trees. Lawyers and government and military officials have come, as well as citizens like me who have paid or otherwise arranged to see the execution of an alleged spy. The journalists were decoyed, I hear; apparently, this is not the usual location for executions at Vincennes. No doubt the more resourceful ones, such as Eric LaPlante, would have discovered a way to penetrate the ruse. If he is here, I don't care; my dealings with that one ended long ago.

I did fulfill my promise to him, but only on condition he never mention my association with Maggie. He never needed to. That little card I gave him launched a lucrative career shadowing the famous dancer.

That's because Mata Hari has been such an object of public interest for all her successes, excesses, and scandals. Her image can still be seen on magazine covers, postcards, posters, cigarette packages, biscuit containers, and many other products. She's been featured in newspapers and magazines countless times. Her father even published a biography, which I did not read.

Each time I encountered her name or face, I would cringe in fear that my full association with her would come out. It never has. Perhaps there is some honour in Eric LaPlante after all, as he kept his promise to me. It's no longer people finding out about my association that might embarrass me, just the discovery of my efforts to conceal it.

A bugle call and the soldiers—a troop of Zouaves, someone told me, only outfitted in conventional uniforms—stand to attention before aligning in formation. From what I gather these poor men have been waiting since two o'clock. They appear rather young. Two rows of six, rifles at their sides, tiny clouds of nervous breath issuing out of mouths every few seconds. To their right, four officers observe solemnly. There is no sound or movement but I know she is approaching.

M'Greet. Maggie. Mata Hari. Convicted spy.

Spy? Oh, she could portray one convincingly enough, of that I'm sure. But to actually function as one? On that point, I must side with the doubters who claim she is a pawn, a dupe, a victim, with an unfortunate predilection for officers, particularly German ones.

She's been many other things though, a friend, a daughter, a mother, a dancer, an actress, a courtesan. Mata Hari's career has risen and fallen many times but her personal life has suffered one constant disappointment. I did make discrete inquiries about her daughter once and discovered the girl's father would fight vigorously any attempt Mata Hari made to see her. Even if I had compromised my own views on the matter to help Maggie, I'd have gotten nowhere. But I never could escape the feeling it wasn't in her daughter's best interest for Maggie to succeed. That was one prejudice I couldn't shake.

Now Mata Hari comes into view, escorted by the sergeant-major who is carrying a blindfold and lanyard. How proud she looks, and lovely still to my eyes, even at forty-one years. She takes a centre-stage position in front of a knoll. The military court captain reads out the pronouncement of her punishment.

The sergeant-major has already looped the rope around her but then pauses before letting it hang loosely, limply around her waist. He produces a blindfold but she shakes her head and says something. He retreats, mumbles something to the young lieutenant, causing a few chuckles from the men. That stops abruptly when the lieutenant raises his sabre, the signal to lift their rifles, which the men do.

The lieutenant turns his attention toward the target. Something she says rattles the officer. And then she lifts her hands, as she might to end a performance, and blows a kiss toward the Zouaves.

The lieutenant lowers his sabre. Twelve rifles discharge their magazines—at least one of which is bound to be blank—and up to eleven bullets fly toward their target. One of the Zouaves faints as the form of Mata Hari crumples to the ground.

"Maggie," I whisper.

The sergeant-major steps forward, pistol at his side, and proceeds to fire a bullet in Mr. Zelle's daughter's head. A real bullet. No spite or malice in the act; it is his duty.

Yet it strikes me as unnecessarily cruel.

Acknowledgements

Leeuwarden's pride in its most famous citizen is evident in the esteem given to Mata Hari in the Fries Museum (www.friesmuseum.nl). I want to express my thanks to curator Evert Kramer for his obliging assistance.

The sources of information about Mata Hari are numerous and differ almost as much on certain details as her own fabricated autobiographies. I found these books helpful in reconciling the facts into my fiction: *The Murder of Mata Hari* by Sam Waagenaar; *Mata Hari, The True Story* by Russell Warren Howe; *Femme Fatale, Love, Lies, and the Unknown Life of Mata Hari* by Pat Shipman; and *Het Meisje Mata Hari* (in Dutch) by H. W. Keikes.

I was lucky while researching this book in the Netherlands, to come across two used books of useful period information: *Zo was Leeuwarden* by Keikes and a Reader's Digest volume called *Nederland Rond 1900*. At the Amsterdam History Museum, I also came upon an interesting and just published book, *De Tweede Gouden Eeuw* (The Second Golden Age), by Frederik H. Kreuger, about Amsterdam between 1880 and 1914. And I often relied on Geert Mak's wonderfully candid, *Amsterdam, A Brief Life of the City*.

A special thank you to my good friend, Anke-Thea Dijkman, for her diligent support. The chapters on Brielle and Rotterdam owe much to her inspiration and encouragement. *Bedankt ook* Ide en Cornelia Kuyper for your kind hospitality. While our meeting was brief, I took from it a genuine sense of Dutch history no book could have provided.

For bravely enduring earlier drafts and offering their helpful opinions, thank you to Henk Hassebroek, Marion Hassebroek, Anna Dykstra, Anne Warman, Trisha Causley, and others.

Of course so much gratitude to my wonderful wife, Yolande, for far more than I can describe in these pages.